Finding Dad

Margaret Pitz

riverrun

Cover Painting: Jillian Banks-Kong

ISBN- 978-0-9888367-0-9

For the people who
encouraged, helped
and supported me
before, during and after:

Carl, Craig, Fran,
Gillie, Hiag, Jim,
John & Mhari,
Justine, and Nick

ONE

'Jessie? Jessie! Are you listening?'

'Yes, Miss.' She wasn't, of course. She rarely did; she knew from experience that she could tune in at the end of the lesson when Miss summarised her main points, and pick up all she needed to pass tomorrow's test. For now she could while away the time thinking about other, more pleasurable and interesting, things. At the moment she was working out whether or not she had actually decided to leave home. Forever.

She didn't know what Miss was on about and she didn't care. Henry the Eighth held no fascination for her, though she did briefly wonder if there were any children involved so when he got rid of one wife somebody's kid ended up with a stepfather who'd smack them about. Henry didn't really look like the smacking type, but maybe ex-Mrs-Henry would move in with somebody like Jock who wouldn't think twice about taking his belt to the kids if he hadn't had a good day. Or even if he had. Or maybe he'd put his dirty rough warty hand down the kid's trousers and then give her a belting when she told her mother – who wouldn't believe her anyway.

'What did I just say?' Miss loomed over Jessie's desk, waiting. Jessie didn't like the feel of her that close. She was skinny and wrinkled, and smelled of old dead flowers mixed with something like the bin, usually overflowing with what looked like bloody bandages, in the public toilets near the market. Jessie slid her eyes to the right where she could just make out Tony mouthing, 'divorced, beheaded, died...'

'Divorced, be'eaded, died, Miss'

'Beheaded. Yes. And then?'

Then? There were more?

'I don't know, Miss. I'm sorry, Miss.' She thought about letting the tears flow but Miss wasn't known to be particularly moved by what she called crocodile tears. Jessie suddenly felt very tired and put her head down on the desk with a sigh.

'All right, Jessie.' Miss sighed too. 'Stay in at break and

write out the whole rhyme five times so you will know.'

'Yes, Miss.'

Miss went back to her desk at the front of the classroom and Jessie went back to her nearly formed decision to run away. It was a shame she'd lost her break, but it didn't really matter. This was very likely the last time she'd ever have to see Miss or any of them again. She was running away. Forever.

It sounded good. She'd tried it out that morning. She'd said, right out of the blue, to the Angel twins, 'I'm going to run away. I'm going to Norwich to live with my dad.' Gabriel and Michael took no notice. They might not have heard her, but she'd heard herself say it out loud and it felt good.

They'd be sorry then, her mum and Jock. Her mum, especially. She'd be sorry she'd accused Jessie of taking money out of the biscuit tin without asking. It wasn't fair. Yes, in the past – only last week actually – she'd helped herself to a few coins, but this time she was innocent. It was probably Jock anyway. He was always taking money out of her mother's purse; he never seemed to have any money of his own. Except when he nicked things out of unlocked cars and then sold them to his mates down the pub. She wished she had taken money now; she was going to need a bit if she was going to run away. And she was. She'd decided now.

•

'Where's our Jess?'

'Don't talk with your mouth full, David.' Milly sounded as automatic as she felt, knowing full well that nothing she said would change either of her children's table manners. David chewed briefly, swallowed, wiped his mouth on his sleeve and asked again: 'Where's our Jess?' He didn't much care, but he did need to make sure she wasn't getting something good that he wasn't getting.

His mother chewed her pursed lips and twisted the resulting knotted mouth to the side. She shrugged.

'Don't know really. P'raps she's stopped to play with her friends.' She wasn't particularly concerned either.

2

If she'd given it any further thought – and she didn't – she would have assumed the ten-year-old would come home if she were hungry. She glanced at Jock. He was busy shovelling jam onto his buttered toast without looking because he was watching the fourth or fifth replay of some mindless footballer's 'amazing! truly amazing – a miracle!' goal. That was all right then. She knew he wouldn't care in principle if Jessie was late for tea but he might make it an excuse to haul off and hit one of them. Or possibly all of them.

'I saw her come out of school,' David volunteered. 'She started walking home but she wasn't with the Angel twins. She went down Summer Lane and they went down Green Road.' He thought this was important enough for some response, but didn't get one. 'Mum?'

Jock looked up. 'I shouldn't worry about her,' he said reasonably enough to David. 'She'll come home when she's ready.'

Jessie's mother felt herself breathe again and sent up a silent prayer to whomever that whatever had come over Jock would stay over him. He could be so nice when he wanted. She smiled lovingly at him but his eyes were firmly on the telly again. Sixth or seventh replay was it? She refilled his tea cup and pushed the plate of toast nearer to him so he could help himself without taking his eyes off the telly.

•

Summer Lane came out into Mortimer Drive, which went nowhere useful for Jessie's purposes, but if you cut through Mrs Windom's garden you could get to the back of the station. But then what? Jessie had no money – how much would it be for a half-fare ticket to Norwich? She did have a plan though, a scheme that she and the Angel twins had used a time or two to get themselves to the local town. It was simple. You rode the train until the conductor asked for your ticket, which you didn't have, of course, then obligingly got off at the next station without paying. You could repeat this, a station at a time, for the four stops to town... but Norwich? Judging by their knowing smiles, the conductors always seemed to know what was going on, but as long as Jessie and her friends got off at the first opportunity, they were usually willing to collude. She wasn't sure she could get away with it for long enough to get to Norwich though. She wasn't even sure the train went to Norwich. In fact, she didn't really have a clear idea of where Norwich actually was. And come to think of it, she also didn't have the foggiest where in Norwich her dad lived.

She decided to get a head start by walking to the next station where she would get on the train to the following stop. She would get off there, walk to the next station and repeat the process till she got to Norwich. She might not get there tonight, but sleeping in the station toilet, or even in the car park – she might find a car unlocked – could be okay she supposed. It would have to be. It could be an adventure. And it would be better than going home. Almost anything would be better than going home to face Jock if her mum had told him – as she'd threatened to do – that Jessie had taken money from the stupid biscuit tin. Jock would know she hadn't, because he had, but that wouldn't stop him giving her a good hiding.

She wished she'd planned better before she'd left home that morning. She wasn't too keen on moving to Norwich wearing her school uniform, and if she'd thought more, she could have packed something to eat along the way. She could have saved something from her school lunch. The tasteless bread roll – that she hadn't eaten but rolled into small pellets to flick at stupid Alice Wilson – would have been quite welcome now. She wondered what they were having for tea at home. Tuesday: might be macaroni and cheese. Or it might be boiled eggs. With toast. And tea. With lots of sugar if no one was looking. She could murder a cup of tea right now.

She was also cold. In her hurry to get away from Gabriel and Michael she'd left her coat at school. Maybe she should go back for it. She stopped in the Windom's garden, hunched up by the fence, and thought about it. School would surely still be open and probably nobody would think it odd that she had come back to get her forgotten coat, if they even saw her. She turned around to go back, but then stopped again. Ahead of her she saw Mrs Windom's weekly wash blowing and swinging in the February breeze. She looked at the possibilities. She certainly didn't want Mr Windom's tee shirts or boxer shorts, and she couldn't think that Mrs Windom's bra would keep her very warm either, huge though it was. But there was a

4

bulky-looking grey sweatshirt with a hood that would do very nicely. She carefully took the pegs off and put them back on the line, moving the towels along a bit to fill the gap she'd created. The sweatshirt was still damp, but it would soon dry and then it would keep her lovely and warm. She turned around again and set off down the garden in the direction of the station once more.

TWO

There were almost too many birds. Or maybe he'd just seen enough for one day. He'd begun just north of King's Lynn, and then followed the A149 around the coast, turning off every time he saw a brown bird sign, and filling in his tick list unbelievably quickly. He thought Cley-next-the-Sea was probably the last spot – it was certainly the last of the day for him, as it was getting too dark to see anything. But how often did he give himself the chance to go birding in Norfolk? Or anywhere else, for that matter. Strictly speaking he didn't have to get back home tonight, not at all – he could find a hotel and continue round the coast tomorrow. Somehow that had more appeal than a long drive back to the Midlands, despite the slight discomfort he always felt when a change of plan was necessary.

'Do you good to be a bit more spontaneous,' he chided himself. 'Thirty-three is much too young to be so old and set in your ways.'

He didn't remember seeing any hotels on his drive today, but then he hadn't been looking for one. In any case, having decided to make another day of it tomorrow, he decided to go on, rather than back. He was fairly sure he'd find something suitable in Cromer, or at least on the way. His spirits rose. A decent hotel, with a bar, room service and some TV in bed – a pleasant way to spend the last night of his birding holiday. He switched from Radio 4 to Radio 3 and began to hum along with the Cockaigne overture.

•

The damp sweatshirt made Jessie feel colder than ever. And it was already getting dark. Even worse, it began to rain. She heard a door bang and to her horror she saw Mrs Windom rushing over to the clothes line to rescue her nowhere-near-dry washing. Jessie crouched down beside the greenhouse and kept as still as she knew how. She hadn't expected rain. Well, she hadn't even thought about it really. Maybe she should wait a bit – she could sit in the greenhouse where she would be warmer and out of the rain. Too bad Mr W didn't have anything useful growing in there she could eat though. Too bad she hadn't packed any warmer clothes, too bad she hadn't thought to bring any food and too bad she hadn't remembered to wear her watch. Actually, she didn't have a watch, but she could have borrowed her mother's without much trouble.

'You just don't think things out, our Jessie,' she could hear Jock passing judgement on her, as he took off his belt to teach her foresight.

Well she'd got some foresight now all right. She could foresee very nicely how much better life was going to be in Norwich, living with her dad. He would want her, he'd be glad to see her after all this time. He wouldn't accuse her of taking money when she hadn't, and he'd understand when she had. He'd be so surprised at how big she was now; she'd been a little kid when he left, a baby really. When she found him she'd curl up in his lap and tell him all the things that had happened since the day he'd walked out for a new life – and a new wife – in Norwich. Her dad would make sure she was always warm and never hungry, and he would never, ever, hit her. She knew that. She'd tell him about Jock hitting her and David and sometimes their mother. She'd tell him about Jock making her mother have a tattoo on her bum when she'd wanted it on her arm, like he had his. Only her mum hadn't wanted to be all covered with them, she'd just wanted a small red rose, not 'Jock's bitch' in dark blue ink. Her dad wouldn't have any tattoos. Or a brown crusted-over earring that made that side of his face smell like the stuff between her toes when she hadn't changed her socks.

So, better get on then. It wasn't raining so much, and in any case the greenhouse had too many panes of glass missing to be anything like dry, so she might as well get going. She knew if she crossed Mortimer Drive she could go through some more gardens and come out onto the main road. Which she assumed would be the right way to Norwich. She set off again.

•

'Jock?'

'What?'

'It's seven o'clock. Do you think Jessie is all right?' Jessie's mum had watched the minutes tick by from ten-to, hoping she wouldn't have to mention her daughter's absence to Jock, and rehearsing what to say that would alert but not alarm him. Or worse, anger him.

'How do I know? Where is she anyway?' He really didn't relish the role of surrogate father to Milly's kids. Why couldn't she take care of them herself and not involve him? He supposed they weren't bad as kids went, not that he'd know, but they were a nuisance, and he was really only interested in Milly and not always that interested in her. Three squares a day, two or three fucks a week – not necessarily with Milly – beer every night and a good game on Saturday, and his life was complete. He might have known she wouldn't come through with her promise to send the kids to live with their dad. He hadn't taken long to realise that she didn't really have any contact with the father of her children – a man who never sent any money. Or if he did, Milly didn't let on, or share it with him. No, he had to live off his wits. Milly's stinginess made him resort to stealing, something he didn't really feel a man like him should have to do. He resented her for that.

'Don't know. She's usually home before this. Shall we go out and look for her?'

'Look for her where? I'm going for a quick one and I seriously doubt she'll be down the pub. If you think she's missing then ring the police. It's their job to find missing kids.'

•

Weybourne was behind him, Sheringham coming up soon. There was very little traffic on the road so it was easy to drive slowly, looking down side roads for any signs of the sort of hotel he had in mind. It was a filthy evening, the sort of drizzle that soaks you through in no time at all and he was pleased all over again with his decision to abandon a dreary drive back to the Midlands.

Just ahead of him, walking slowly, was a slight figure, hunched over. He couldn't tell if it was a boy or a girl, but something about the way he or she was walking made him slow down to look. The small body seemed so depressed somehow.

'Don't be daft,' he reproved himself. 'You can't tell from the way somebody walks that they're depressed.' He slowed down a little more and turned to look as he drove by. He still couldn't

8

tell if it was a boy or a girl – did it matter? Well, yes… but he could see from the facial expression that he hadn't been mistaken about the sadness.

He drove on a little way then, at the roundabout, he went all the way around and drove back toward the small figure. There was no one about, and as far as he could tell, there were no CCTV cameras on this stretch of road. Where on earth could this kid be going all by him or herself? And so inadequately dressed for a cold and rainy early February evening. He drove past again, turned around once more in the Little Chef he'd just recently passed and then pulled up alongside the stooped over child.

'Are you all right?' He had rolled down the window on the passenger side but was careful not to lean too far forward and appear threatening.

It was a girl. She had stopped when he stopped. 'Yes thank you.' It was a very sweet voice.

'It's a nasty night – can I give you a lift somewhere?'

'No thank you.' Was it a reluctant refusal? Or was he just indulging in a bit of wishful thinking?

'I know it's not a good idea to accept lifts from strangers, but I am, I promise you, a very nice man and I'm only offering because you look so down in the dumps – and wet.'

'And cold.' She stared at her feet.

'It's lovely and warm in my car…' No response. 'Where are you going?'

'Norwich. I'm going to live with my dad.'

'Lucky dad! What's his name?'

'Um…' She didn't know.

'What's your name then? Mine's Will.'

'Jessie.'

'Jessie eh? Do you think it suits you? I think Will suits me – I chose it.'

'What do you mean? People get their names when they're

9

babies. You couldn't choose your name then.' She moved a little closer to the car window. She was interested.

'Well yes, they do. But I was given a name I didn't like, so when I had a chance to change it, I chose Will. I named myself after a man I really admire. Would you like a different name?'

'I dunno. I might...' She sounded doubtful.

'What name would you like for you?'

'I don't know all the names in the world. My best friend's called Gabriel but he's a boy and I don't want a boy's name. My other best friend is called Michael. They're twins, you know.'

'No, I didn't know. Must be fun to have twins for friends. Won't they miss you if you go to Norwich?'

'They might. I've got to go now.'

'Well it's been very nice to meet you Jessie. Are you sure I can't buy you a drink of hot chocolate before you struggle on? I'm going to get one for myself and it would be a pleasure to get one for you too.'

'No thank you.' The prim, don't-talk-to-strangers tone had returned.

'Okay. Well, all the best then.' He moved slowly on, wondering if he'd given up too soon. Watching her in the rear view mirror, he thought she wasn't exactly in a hurry to move on herself.

He turned left down a side street, then left and left again, noting again the absence of cameras, and coming out by the Little Chef, where he bought a coffee and a hot chocolate to take away. There were CCTV cameras in the car park, but he couldn't see any further on, out in the road. He didn't think Jessie would have gone far, not at the rate she was moving, but he hurried all the same whilst trying not to spill the drinks.

Indeed she hadn't gone far, and he thought she seemed pleased when he pulled up beside her again.

'I brought you a hot chocolate drink anyway. Here!' he offered it through the window to her. She stepped forward and took it, just as he'd thought she would.

THREE

'The police weren't all that bothered,' Milly told her neighbour, who'd come round to see if there'd been any news. 'They think she's playing with her friends but if she doesn't come home by ten o'clock they said we should ring up again.'

'I suppose they're a bit fed up with fetching your kids back from the bus station.' Agnes wasn't one to mince her words.

'I wouldn't say my kids,' Milly sniffed, 'Jessie's never done anything like that. David's sort of run away a time or two, only hung round the bus station really, but Jessie never has. I don't think she's run away now either. But she's going to get it when she does come home – from me and 'im.'

'Well if you want any help to go looking for her, me 'n' Les'll go out with you.'

It wouldn't come to that, surely. Milly couldn't believe that Jessie would run away from home just because she'd been accused of taking money without asking. In any case, she knew now that Jessie hadn't taken the money out of the biscuit tin – Jock had – so running away, what a guilty person would do, wouldn't make any sense. But then where was she? She knew better than to stay out past bedtime. She wasn't playing with anyone Milly knew, either, because she'd phoned round to ask.

Milly didn't know what to think. Jock had gone down the pub as usual and when pressed had said he would keep an eye out for Jessie, but he hadn't seemed concerned. In fact, he seemed to think it was funny. Milly didn't. She was annoyed and took the opportunity to snap at David when he didn't move fast enough to start getting himself off to bed.

It was David who said it out loud. 'Maybe somebody's kidnapped her.'

•

He almost laughed out loud He would have but for fear of waking Jessie, curled up on the passenger seat as close to the door as she could get, her seatbelt so loose it was hardly functional. An hour ago he was exulting at the prospect of another night in Norfolk to avoid a long drive home; now he was steaming down the A148, heading for King's Lynn, Peterborough, Leicester, Tamworth and home. And while he wasn't exactly exulting, he was feeling very, very pleased with himself.

Jessie had resisted, but not too vigorously. She hadn't wanted to sit in the car to drink her chocolate, but had not objected when he got out and stood with her inside the nearby bus shelter, drinking his coffee. Conversation hadn't exactly flowed. He established that she was 'ten-nearly-eleven', and liked watching Neighbours and The Simpsons, but it was hard going.

'Good? Your chocolate drink, I mean?' His coffee was foul but the steam from her hot chocolate wafting past his face smelled quite pleasant.

'Yes thank you,' very primly. Another long silence, then 'How far is it to Norwich from here?'

'Too far to walk. I could give you a lift but I have to go somewhere else first. If you'd trust me and go with me, I could take you to Norwich later if you like.'

More silence. Then, 'Or you could give me the train money and I could go straight away.'

'Well, no, I can't do that – I never carry any money. People don't these days, you know. I was lucky to find enough loose change in the car for the drinks, actually. And by the time I'd found a cash machine that's working we could have done my errand and be on our way to Norwich.'

'I'm not supposed to get in anybody's car.'

'But I'm not anybody. You know me now. I'm Will, I bought you a drink. If I'd wanted to hurt you I wouldn't be squatting here on this incredibly uncomfortable bench, enjoying your company now, would I?'

More silence.

'Would you like to use my phone and ring your dad?' He'd

taken a chance but instinct told him what her response would be.

'I don't know his number.'

'We can get it from something called Directory Enquiries if you like. What's his name?'

'It's… I think it's… I don't remember.' Her look of total tragedy had torn at his insides. Did she even know where he lived?

She did not. She knew he lived in Norwich because her Mum had said so, she thought, but she didn't know his address. He'd raised the stakes a little.

'Well then I think you'd better come with me on my errand and then we can take all the time we need to find him in Norwich. I think you're going to need me to help you do that, you know.' All the conflict had flitted across her face. He'd waited.

'Okay then,' she'd said finally, and immediately climbed into the passenger seat, leaving her chocolate cup on the pavement. Hardly able to believe his luck he picked up her cup, dropped it with his into the bin inside the bus shelter, and walked round to the driver's side and got in

'Okay then it is. My errand first though. Make yourself as comfortable as you can inside the seatbelt. We don't want to be stopped for breaking the law.' They had both laughed and then there was silence. He thought she fell asleep almost right away but he couldn't be sure at first.

He was sure now though, and he hoped she would stay asleep for the whole night. He could deal better with the next step in the morning.

•

Milly, Jock, Agnes and Les had a dreadful night. Under instructions from the police they had first combed the area, up and down each street and alleyway, yelling for Jessie and complaining to each other about how cold it was. Nobody thought about how cold it might be for Jessie, until the policewoman assigned as their liaison brought it up. By then the school had been searched and Jessie's coat had been found, heightening concern, but nobody was impressed by Jock's anger at his stepdaughter's carelessness.

All Jessie's known friends' and schoolmates' parents had been contacted. David had been questioned for what had seemed like hours – until he just couldn't stop shaking and crying, and he could no longer speak. At that point the policewoman made them all a cup of tea and the sergeant in charge, after consulting with his superior, said they had to make a media announcement about a missing child.

Milly was shocked. Surely not? Surely Jessie was just playing up and would be home soon? Jock wasn't shocked but he did agree with Milly and let everyone within earshot know just what would happen when she did get home. This led to an entirely different line of questioning, which in turn led to David's confession that he, too, had often thought of running away and trying to find his dad.

Did David think Jessie had gone to find her dad? Had she ever said anything like that? David didn't think so, but she might have said something to her friends; which in turn led to an early morning interview with Gabriel and Michael in which, eventually, Gabriel volunteered that just that morning (yesterday, actually) she'd said she was going to Norwich to live with her dad.

'Her dad doesn't live in Norwich!' Milly was aghast when the policeman passed on this bit of news. 'He lives in Newcastle, or somewhere up there.'

'All the same,' the stern-faced policeman said, 'we'll need to alert the Norwich police. And I suppose the Newcastle and district police too.' He sighed. If he'd been unlucky enough to be a child in this family he'd have hiked to the ends of the earth if he thought he'd find a decent dad there. He shook himself mentally. 'Mustn't judge... follow procedures and hope for the best.' He tried not to think the next line of the well-worn mantra. He didn't want to fear the worst.

FOUR

Crikey! Whose bed was this? Where on earth was she? Jessie sat up in a panic and looked around. It wasn't her room. For one thing, it was much too clean and tidy. And for another it was a big bed instead of her rickety old camp bed. Was she at her dad's? How had she got there? And if not her dad's, then whose house was this and whose bed was she in?

She looked around the room, hoping for clues. Nothing on the bedside table; nothing on top of the chest of drawers. There was a small bookcase under the window, filled with a row of identical dark blue books. By squinting hard, she could just make out the beginning of the title – the same on each one: The Story of Civ-something, she couldn't manage the final word.

She suddenly remembered the man, and how she'd got into the car to go with him on his errand so they could go to Norwich afterwards and find her dad. She didn't remember the errand but she vaguely remembered him stopping somewhere and getting fish and chips for them both. Had she eaten hers? Probably not, she was pretty hungry now.

Was this the man's house?

'Only one way to find out,' she told herself firmly, and slid out of bed, still fully dressed in her school uniform, including her socks. The grey sweatshirt was neatly folded on the chair beside the huge double bed and her scruffy brown shoes were parked tidily side by side underneath it.

There were three doors in the room, all painted stark white like the walls: which one was the way out? She tried the one next to the window through which she could see nothing she could identify. No clues about where she was, except that it wasn't anywhere she'd seen before, she was pretty sure of that. There were fields as far as the eye could see, and what looked like some cows a long way off in the distance, but no sea and no houses. That door wouldn't open, so she tried the one on the other side of the room. It opened into a bathroom, which she suddenly realised she was very glad to find. She used the toilet but didn't bother washing herself. She looked at herself in the mirror over the shiny white sink. Her short, reddish-brown hair was rumpled and dirty looking. Her freckled face looked pretty grubby, even to her, but she didn't feel like doing anything about it, even though she noticed, touched and briefly admired, the thick fluffy yellow facecloth on the sink and the matching towels on the rail beside the equally shiny white bath. Personal hygiene wasn't high on Jessie's list of essentials.

The third door, next to the bathroom, opened into a cupboard containing nothing but file boxes, stacked floor to ceiling. Each one was labelled. Jessie was a pretty good reader, second best in her class, next to Tony Walton, but these letters and numbers were meaningless to her.

She returned to the bed and sat on it, puzzled. Should she bang on the door, or shout? Could she climb out of the window? And if she could, what would she do then? Perhaps she should try the first door again; maybe it was stuck. She turned the knob and rattled it. It opened almost immediately, and there was the man, standing in the hall outside.

'Good morning,' he smiled. 'You look as if you slept well. Would you like some breakfast?'

She would. And then she'd like to get on and find her dad in Norwich please. She said as much.

'Yes, of course. Let's have our breakfast and work out a plan for the day.' He led the way downstairs and into the kitchen where the table was already laid for two, with cereal bowls, plates, knives and spoons, and a well-filled toast rack. Jessie didn't wait to be asked; she took a piece of toast and began slathering it with butter, then jam.

She looked around the kitchen. The walls were plain white, just like the ones in the bedroom. Apart from a calendar with various coloured marks in some of the squares, there was nothing to relieve the vast expanse of white. Jessie stared at the spaces, wondering if she liked the peace of them after the clutter that crowded every inch of wall space in her own home in Sheringham. She did like the scrubbed pine table with its brightly coloured chairs, each one different. Apart from these two impressions, the rest of the room was just a kitchen to her. She concentrated on her second piece of toast.

'Hungry, eh? You must be, you didn't eat much last night.'

Jessie looked at him as she ate. He was old, of course, but probably not much older than Jock. He had nice dark hair curling round the bottom of his ears, and brown eyes; and his teeth, when he smiled, were straight and white. Jessie admired men with nice teeth, probably because Jock's were so rotten and black looking. Yesterday evening, she remembered, the man had been wearing a green and black striped shirt and a dark red zipped-up jacket. This morning he had on a yellow checked shirt with a cable knit brown jumper over it. His dark green trousers were corduroy, Jessie thought, but she wasn't sure. Whatever, she quite liked what she saw. She didn't think he was particularly tall but he was, she considered, a bit handsome. All in all, she thought, nodding to herself, she quite approved of his appearance and his bright warm kitchen. Hopefully her dad's house would be as nice.

'Penny for your thoughts?'

'What?' she frowned, not knowing what he meant.

'I was wondering what you were thinking, but it's actually quite rude of me to ask. I'm sure you'll tell me anything you want me to know.' He filled his cereal bowl with cornflakes then, cocking his head on one side, said, 'You?' and in response to her silent nod, poured flakes into her bowl.

'Are we near Norwich?' Jessie was enjoying her breakfast all right, but felt she needed to keep him on track. He was nice enough, but he wasn't her dad and although she wasn't exactly missing her mother – and certainly not Jock – she was feeling a need to be with some kind of family. It would be safer, she told herself.

'It's not too far. But look here, I can't take you to your dad looking like that. I think we need to get you some clean clothes before we go. Let's go into town this morning and buy you something clean, something you like, and then after lunch we'll go to Norwich.'

Jessie was torn. She didn't often get the offer of new clothes and never with the promise that it would be something she liked. She knew she was crumpled looking, and she'd never liked her school uniform so she'd be happy not to find her dad while she was wearing it. But it would delay them and she didn't want that. She ate the cornflakes and helped herself to yet another piece of toast whilst she made up her mind.

'All right then,' she decided, 'then we'll go straight to Norwich.' She used her firmest voice so there'd be no misunderstanding.

•

Will felt very pleased at the way things were going. The child was understandably a bit on edge, but it seemed reasonably easy to reassure her and get her cooperation. She had washed her face and combed her hair with no resistance. She had even cleaned her teeth, once he produced a new toothbrush for her. The next bit might be trickier; he would need to explain her presence if they met anyone in Lichfield who knew him, and he'd need her support for any story he made up. He decided to go for the truth.

'You're a with-it little girl, Jessie,' he began as they drove towards the city, 'so you'll understand when I say that some people might think it a bit odd for a man to be out with a young girl, especially if he's buying her clothes.' He looked quickly at her and saw that she was listening, even though she wasn't taking her eyes off the road as they drove along. 'So I thought we could say you're my niece, visiting me for a day or two until,' he had a sudden brainwave, 'until you go to Norwich to stay with your dad.' He looked at her again. 'Okay?'

'Okay.' She looked at the road sign. 'Lick-field two miles. Is that near Norwich?'

'Near enough. And it's pronounced Lichfield.' Of course a ten-year-old wouldn't have much sense of geography. He smiled to himself. She'd probably never heard of Lichfield or the Midlands. Her world seemed to extend no further than Sheringham. And Norwich, of course, though possibly not even that far.

They parked in the Frog Lane car park and walked down the precinct to a suitable-looking shop he'd remembered next to Boots, stopping at the cash point briefly. The city wasn't crowded. Years ago Wednesday had been early closing day and the habit of not coming into town on a Wednesday had stuck, even with younger people who didn't know what 'early closing day' meant. All the same, he was on edge and hoped they were inconspicuous.

He needn't have worried. They met nobody who recognised him because in fact he didn't really know anybody. And certainly not to speak to. He wasn't a regular anywhere, shopping in Lichfield, Tamworth, Birmingham, Burton, and occasionally London, as the mood took him. He had his hair cut in different places or hacked it off himself. And Jessie was far too involved with choosing the clothes to make small talk with the shop girl – who wasn't that interested in them anyway. She let them pick out a jumper, a blouse and two pairs of trousers because Jessie couldn't decide which she preferred, all the time talking on her mobile phone and only breaking off long enough to suggest Marks & Spencer's in response to his diffident enquiry about underwear. If she'd wondered how come this little girl was visiting her uncle in her dishevelled school uniform and needed new everything, she certainly didn't show it. Will felt reasonably sure they hadn't registered on her memory banks at all.

M&S was much the same story. Underwear didn't interest Jessie much anyway, so Will picked up a bundle of socks, a packet of vests and another of knickers, paid for them and they were done. He decided against new shoes for the moment; he could polish these into some kind of respectability, he thought.

'Can I go in their Ladies and change, then?' Jessie was evidently keeping her eye on the correct order of things.

'Ah, yes… er, no, let's find a nice café where we can get some tea or chocolate and perhaps a piece of cake and you can use their Ladies Room to change.' Will felt he needed fortifying before tackling the next 'let's get on to Norwich then'.

But he'd underestimated her tenacity. 'No, I want to go to Norwich now.' Will suddenly realised that in Jessie's experience the way to get what you wanted was to just keep on about it. 'I can change really fast and then we can get going.'

'I know you're anxious to go. But…' Will searched for another delaying tactic. 'Oh, you know, I didn't want to tell you this but I have a sort of illness. I have to eat something every couple of hours or so or I get so weak I might faint. So I'm sorry, but we have to stop for a snack.'

Jessie looked horrified, but didn't argue. Will could see she wouldn't want to be driving round Norwich looking for her dad with a man who might faint. She didn't care about him particularly, he knew that, but he also knew that she was well aware that for the moment her future was in his hands. And they'd better be safe ones.

•

Jessie began to feel a bit better when they stopped at WH Smith so that Will could buy a street map of Norwich. He gave her three pounds and told her to go into the bakery next door for Eccles cakes, which Will said they would eat in the car. That would be good – at least they would be on their way and not sitting in some dumb coffee shop for another hour or more. Perhaps she could sit in the back and change there. She didn't know whether to suggest that, she didn't know if she felt all right about doing that anyway. So she got in the front and munched on her Eccles cake as they drove. After about fifteen minutes they slowed to a halt and with a brief pause Will made a careful left turn into a driveway.

'Hey, we're back at your house. I thought we were going to Norwich.' The panic began to rise.

'We are – going to Norwich, I mean. But not till you've had a bath and put your new clothes on. I don't want to deliver you to your dad looking like you've been pulled through a hedge backwards, as they say.'

Jessie sighed. He was just like all the other grownups. But she conceded he had a point, and in any case, she was quite keen to look her best in her new clothes. It was the first time in her life she had actually chosen an outfit for herself and she thought she'd done a pretty good job.

He showed her how to run the bath and gave her some lavender oil to put in it. Then he took her shoes to clean and left her to it. She locked the door behind him. He was all right, but you never quite knew.

She'd never before enjoyed a bath as much as she enjoyed this one. In fact, she didn't think she'd ever actually enjoyed a bath before. She almost forgot she was in a hurry to get moving. But remember she did, eventually, so she dried herself quickly on the fluffy yellow towel and put on her new underwear and then the bright blue-and-white striped blouse, navy trousers and jumper, and finally the socks with Wallace and Grommet on the front. Her dad would be so proud of his daughter.

Should she take the school uniform with her? And what about the Windom's sweatshirt? She couldn't imagine needing any of it again, so she just left it all where she'd dropped it before her bath and went into the kitchen to tell Will she was ready.

He was frying chips. Well, that was all right, she could never get tired of chips, but when were they going to get going and start looking round Norwich? She sensed somehow it was pointless to ask now, so settled down to enjoy her eggs and chips; she'd start nagging again later.

FIVE

'...has been missing for a full week now and police say they still have no clues. Hundreds of houses in the area have been searched, dozens of people have been interviewed, divers have been searching ponds and ditches in the area and several dozen posters of Jessie have been handed out in Sheringham, Cromer, Norwich and other major centres as far north as Tyne and Wear and Northumberland. No trace of Jessie or her whereabouts has been found. Despite receiving over 300 phone calls from people with information to offer, nothing has turned up a single clue so far. In a press conference this morning, police spokesman Peter Ferguson said that although they were still looking for a missing little girl, they must also consider the possibility that Jessie was dead. Or that she had fallen into some wrong hands. They would not be giving up the search. Her family is said to be...'

Cursing softly Will switched it off. He knew they couldn't just give up and accept they weren't going to find her. And he knew they needed the media to help them. He didn't mind the police searching – it wouldn't come to anything and the police needed to be seen to be doing something after all – but he'd be glad when they shifted to behind-the-scenes work and stopped putting items about it on the news. It was interfering with his plans to get Jessie up to speed on current affairs so that they could have intelligent discussions together. There was a lot of interesting activity in the world these days, what with the usual posturing in the Middle East – he longed to talk to her about that and his ideas for a better, more civilised way, of being – the ever-present political circus in America, the dangerously deteriorating state of the environment. But he daren't risk having the news on yet in case she saw her mother – or worse, her dad – making an emotional appeal for her to come home. So for a while longer at least, his views on civilisation would have to wait and they were stuck with watching Countdown, or tennis and cricket. But he could be patient and meantime, since she had known nothing about either sport, there was plenty of educating Jessie to get on with.

She was an eager and quick learner. Sometimes the questions

she asked about the finer points of cricket, for example, staggered him – he didn't know the answer. But together they'd look it up in Wisden or online; he was also teaching her the value of knowing where to look things up, and how to do so.

He shook the jar that contained his vitamins and emptied three into his hand. Great! Second day in a row that the three different ones he took daily – and no others – had come out of the jar. He put a small red tick on the calendar next to the blue tick that indicated he'd slept all night without having to get up to relieve himself. No green tick – yet, of course. The day wasn't over. He might get a green tick by bedtime, assuming he did manage to eat his five portions of fruit and vegetables. He didn't always, but keeping track this way helped him keep an eye on it. He liked to look back over a whole month and count how many days he'd achieved his goal. And, happily, no black cross either. He knew he'd never forget what each colour and symbol signified, but maybe he should do a small key and attach it to the back of the calendar anyway, just in case. Actually, that would be a nice little task for Ariel, as he'd begun calling her in his mind, long before he'd caught sight of the small figure, bent almost double against the persistent drizzle on the Sheringham Road.

•

Days were going by and they never seemed to be going to Norwich. It was always too late, or Will was too tired, or too hungry, or he had something else he had to do. He never said they weren't going, but it just wasn't happening. In Jessie's experience this sort of 'we'll see' attitude in a grown up could mean either it never will happen, or, if you kept on long enough, they'd give in. She couldn't work out which this would be. She still wanted to get to Norwich and find her dad, of course she did, but in truth she was actually having a pretty good time with Will. The thought crossed her mind that living with dad might not be as good. Might, in fact, be a whole lot worse. But she was nothing if not stubborn. Her end of term school report had said so, right after the statement that 'Jessie should pay more attention to her own work and less to other children's paintings' – giving Jock another excuse to slap her. He'd assumed, like Miss had, that she'd been copying, but she hadn't; she'd been admiring, that's all. Her frustrated indignation was all the harder to bear because, for once, in her eyes, she wasn't in the wrong.

She'd enjoyed looking at the street map of Norwich, though as far as she was concerned it might just as well have been a street map of Mars. Except she didn't think they had streets on Mars yet. Will had patiently pointed out various 'landmarks', as he called them, and showed her where the streets were listed in alphabetical order and how to find one on the map itself. She liked doing that sort of thing with him. Actually she liked doing anything with him. She liked the attention and she liked his approval and praise. Yesterday, when she'd said 'Why have they gone in with five bowlers and only four batsmen then?' while they were watching the cricket from India, he'd ruffled her hair and said,

'You little sweetheart!'

She hadn't liked to tell him she was only saying what she'd heard Nasser Hussain say five minutes earlier, while Will was in the kitchen. Nor did she want to ask him how four plus five could add up to the eleven she knew was needed for a cricket side. There was a wicketkeeper, yes, but still that was only ten. Oh well, probably there was one who did a bit of everything.

Making the colour key for his ticks and symbols had been fun, too. He'd only explained what the red tick meant – telling her to leave a blank beside the others for now – so she had watched him carefully for the past two mornings when he'd shaken out his three vitamins, and crowed with delight this morning when the correct three – and only the correct three – had emerged into his waiting hand. He'd let her put the red tick on the calendar and she felt such pride in his achievement. Later he'd let her refill the jar with 20 each of the three tablets and tried to explain to her what the chances were – 'odds', he called it – of getting only the three he wanted. She liked the term 'odds' but couldn't even say statistics, though she quite approved of the concept, and readily accepted his insistence that she must put 20 of each in, no more and no less, nodding solemnly and counting each group twice to be sure. He'd shown some surprise that she could count to 20 and she'd taken great pleasure in demonstrating her scorn that there might be people in his world who couldn't do even that.

He was quite the nicest teacher she'd ever had. He never got cross. When they made a mistake (well, when she made a mistake) on the Sudoku he just said: 'Let's go back over it and see where we went wrong – sometimes that's as satisfying as getting it right first time.' They did the Killer Sudoku each morning over breakfast; Will read the Times online then printed off the puzzles and the cryptic crossword. She wasn't getting anywhere with understanding that concept, but she liked the way he encouraged her to try, and explained things to her. They sat side by side at the kitchen table and she enjoyed the clean and soapy smell of him. She wasn't really any good at the polygon – or Countdown – either, but Will would point to the letters in order and help her spell out a word. He'd been really pleased with himself yesterday when he got twenty-one words out of the jumble of letters, and said that was his record. He showed her where to write twenty-one on the calendar for yesterday and again she felt so proud of him.

•

Three weeks and still not a trace. Dozens, hundreds of police were working on it and people were still being questioned but all to no avail, the police kept telling the media – whose interest had flagged considerably over the past few days. They had other, more exciting, fish to fry. Some human remains – a bone, too large and too weathered to be the missing Jessie – had been found by fishermen in the waters off the Western Isles.

Agnes, whose house had already been thoroughly searched twice, turning up an embarrassing cache of soft porn magazines in Les's garden shed, was now giving shelter to Milly, Jock and David whilst their house was turned inside out and upside down. And wondering where she'd ever got the idea that they were pretty decent people.

'He's not just nasty to David,' she said to Les, 'He's downright cruel. Fancy telling a nine-year-old he'll never pull a bird if he doesn't stop wetting the bed!'

'Well he probably won't.' Les was fed up with dodging sheets drying on the line every day, impeding his progress in the garden where he was nurturing the soil in which he planned to grow some prize-winning leeks.

'Still an' all, I don't suppose Jock's making it any better for any of them.' Les had never taken to Jock, partly because he'd liked having Milly living next door as a single mother. He'd enjoyed helping her mend this and sort that, and he often wished he'd asked Milly to come with him to the village dance all those years ago, instead of Agnes. Who knows how things would have worked out if he had. Agnes was all right – they'd become sort of used to each other – but there was something about Milly's lithe little body and her still-pert tits that made him feel warm and tingly under his boxer shorts in a way that he'd never experienced with Agnes. Not even in their earliest days of groping each other behind the clubroom kitchen, when Agnes's tits had already melded into one solid lump of clammy flesh.

''Ere!' he said to Agnes, suddenly excited, 'You don't think Jock's done away with her, do you?' He himself didn't think so for a minute, but he liked the idea of getting Jock off the scene if he could, even if only temporarily. Comforting Milly in Jock's absence was an exciting prospect to Les.

'Funny you should say that,' Agnes moved closer to him and whispered wetly in his ear, 'Milly's told me the police, especially that spotty-faced fat sergeant, keeps asking her if she thinks Jock might be glad that Jessie's gone. They think he done it, she's sure of it.'

'Well I never... Does Milly think he has?' Les hadn't expected this.

'You never know what Milly's thinking, Les. You know that.' Agnes knew that Les had always fancied Milly. Though she didn't think he knew she knew. In her odd and angry way, Agnes dearly loved the short, balding Les and almost couldn't believe her luck that she'd got him to the altar first, before Milly had seemed to even notice his existence. She hadn't minded when Milly and Howard and their two kids had moved in next door, though she hadn't been happy when Howard walked out after less than two years. Les had been far too accommodating with Milly's helpless little woman needs, to her way of thinking. So, oh the relief when the exhausted single mother took up with the surly, ferret-faced Jock – who made it quite clear that this was now his territory, thank you very much.

'No, you're not wrong there missus.' Les sighed. He hoped Milly was thinking along the same lines as him, but Agnes was right, you never did know what went on in that little head of hers.

SIX

'What kind of music do you like?' Her choice of television programmes appalled him: Neighbours, Coronation Street, EastEnders. He'd tried to watch them with her, to be companionable, but it hadn't been easy. Her absolute pre-Will favourite was apparently The Simpsons, which they hadn't watched together yet, but he felt fairly sure he wasn't going to like it when – if – they did. He was hoping he wouldn't have to humour her that far.

'Dunno. Leona Lewis? My mum likes some boy bands but I don't.'

'Let's listen to something I like – it's a piece of what's called 'programme music'. What that means is that there is a story that goes with it. I'll tell you the story as we listen to it and you can imagine the scene. All right?'

'Okay.'

He knew she meant it – so far she had found everything enjoyable that he had introduced her to, probably because they did it together and he explained anything she didn't understand as they went along. Her short life seemed to have consisted of nothing but negative attention, if any. He felt sad about that; she was a nice child and seemed, to his inexperienced eye, unusually bright. She certainly seemed to thoroughly enjoy learning about anything he cared to teach her. Well it would be different from now on. They would do more and more of things like this, and sooner or later, hopefully sooner, they would begin their life's work together, their civilisation and history writing. He felt a warm benevolent glow creeping up his torso.

'It's called Pictures at an Exhibition, and it's by a composer named Modest Mussorgsky. He was Russian – that means he came from the country called Russia –I'll show you on the map in a minute. He went to an exhibition of paintings that had been done by a friend of his named Viktor Hartmann. He liked the exhibition so much that he went home and wrote a little piece of music about each picture. And in between each one he put what he calls 'promenade' music to show he is walking from one painting to the next.' He watched her taking it all in, her greenish-hazel eyes flicking repeatedly from his face to the CD player and back again, her mouth twitching with anticipation.

He started the CD, pausing it before each section to tell her what the picture was about.

'This is my favourite. It's called Bydlo in Polish, that's Polish for ox, and the painting shows the ox coming back to the farm after working in the fields all day.'

'Working? What did he do?'

He smiled – he could see she had a cartoon-style vision of a large bull digging or something similar.

'He pulls the plough that digs up the earth. He's very strong but it's hard work and probably boring, and he's very tired at the end of a long day of doing that. So he plods home very, very slowly – hear? – then he gets to the top of the hill and he can smell his barn and he goes faster and faster because he wants to be home to have his supper and because it's easier going downhill. Listen…' He watched her face and felt she was liking what she heard. He was certainly liking what he saw.

At the end of the CD he asked her which bit she had liked best.

'That flying chicken shed thing. Creepy! But in a good way.' She shuddered.

'Chicken shed? Do you mean The Hut on Fowl's Legs?' She nodded. 'It is creepy sounding isn't it? Let's hear that bit again. I like it too, and I especially like the way it moves into the Great Gate of Kiev to end the piece. Can't you just see the magnificent city gate?'

He got so much pleasure from teaching her, from sharing his knowledge, such as it was. (She may have thought he knew everything but he had no illusions.) And his pleasure was heightened by her obvious pleasure at learning. He wanted to go on and on, but cautioned himself to be careful, she was only ten after all, and did not have the attention span of a fifteen-year-old. Yet she learned so quickly and so well that it was hard not to push. He was so hungry for intellectual stimulation and he'd waited so long… But he mustn't make a mistake this time. He must take all the time it needed to bring her up to the point of being his equal. And then, ah then… they could do so much together. Will and Ariel. He sighed. Third time lucky, as they say.

•

The clothes they'd bought in Lichfield were nice, but she was a bit tired of wearing the same thing day after day. And she was very tired of sleeping in the Windom's capacious grey sweatshirt. Should she mention it to Will? Come to think of it, he seemed a bit peeved at having to run the washing machine all the time to keep up with her need for clean underwear. Well, strictly speaking it wasn't her need, it was his, but the end result was the same. She only had four sets so he had to do a load of washing more often than he probably wanted.

While she was wondering how to raise the issue, he brought it up. He appeared in the kitchen with a large cardboard box she recognised as having come out of the cupboard in her room. It was the one labelled A-II Apparel. 'You need some more clothes really. These might be too big for you, but on the other hand there might be something in here you can wear. Do you want to have a look?'

She did. She opened the large box and found dresses, jumpers, skirts, socks, shorts, underwear and tops galore. Best of all there were pyjamas and a dressing gown. 'Whose are these then?' She worried that the owner of this lot might not like her wearing them.

'They belonged to a cousin who visited, but she won't be needing them. She'd be happy for you to have them, I'm sure. If you like them.'

She did like them. Mostly she liked having a selection and although most of the items were on the big side, she knew she could find enough in the box to give her a change, several changes. She tugged on the orange tee shirt. It was big, but big didn't matter in a tee shirt.

'I love it! Can I really have it?'

'Yes you may, not can.' But he smiled. 'I think I can find

another box with shoes and things, too. Take them to your room and put them away and wear them as and when you like. Put them in neat stacks in your drawer and when you get clean – or new – ones, remember to put them underneath so everything gets used in proper order.'

Using things in proper order seemed very important to Will. A few days ago he had ordered – and received – a packet of eight multi-coloured handkerchiefs. Together they had admired the various designs and she had wanted him to put them in his drawer stacked in order of preference. And of course on the top of the pile already there, so he could use them right away.

'How can you bear to wait?' she'd asked, but Will had shaken his head, replaced them in the order they had come out of the packet and put them under the existing stack.

'Waiting for things makes them even better when they finally come along,' he'd said with a smile. 'Anticipation is often the best part of any event.' He always put the clean sheets, towels, facecloths away under the current pile in the linen cupboard. The same with the tea towels in the drawer in the kitchen, and when Jessie had pulled out a bright red one from the middle of the stack he'd asked her to put it back and use the boring blue and white one that was on the top.

'Things have to be used in their proper order,' he'd said. It was the same with food, even things like tins of baked beans. Tins already in the cupboard were to be pulled to the front and the newly bought ones piled in – neatly, of course – at the back. Jessie didn't really mind, though she did find it hard to remember all the time. But as with everything else, Will showed her almost unlimited patience about it all, so she was more than willing to give it a go. When she remembered.

'Will your cousin mind if she comes back and finds her clothes gone?' Jessie knew she'd mind a lot, and couldn't imagine another girl not minding.

'She won't be coming back, I'm afraid.' He looked serious.

'Why not?' Jessie couldn't understand someone choosing not to return to visit Will.

'Well, I'm afraid she's dead. But please don't let that stop your enjoyment of the clothes – I'm sure it would have made her very happy.'

Jessie wasn't so sure. The idea of the cousin being dead shocked her a little, but she did want the clothes so decided she was prepared to overlook the matter. After all, she probably hadn't actually died wearing any of these things. 'What's her name then, your cousin?'

'Um, Ari... um Sally.' He seemed odd. Jessie thought there was probably a better word for it, but 'odd' would have to do. He was probably still a bit upset about Cousin Sally's death.

'What did she die of?' Jessie wasn't upset but she was curious.

'I don't really know – she wasn't here then, it was over a year ago. Don't worry, I'm over it really. I suppose it was just bringing out her clothes that brought it back. But please, don't worry. Let's do the washing up and then we'll go for a birding walk. There isn't much at this time of year but I want you to be able to recognise what is here now, and then you'll notice when the new ones start arriving in the spring. We have so much to look forward to, you and I. Let's not think about death.'

Jessie had moved on almost before he'd finished speaking. Going birding was the latest new and interesting activity he'd introduced her to. Life with Will was great. She hardly ever thought about Sheringham now.

SEVEN

'When will you be eleven, Jessie?'

'On my next birthday.'

Will smiled. The unexpectedness of some of her answers never failed to touch him. 'Of course, and when is that?'

'The fifth of March.'

'Lord, Jessie, that's tomorrow! We must celebrate! I already know what your main present will be, but we must do something special – eleven is a very significant milestone.' Thanks heavens he'd thought to ask her today. It would have been an anti-climax if he'd found out after her birthday that the magic milestone had passed without notice.

He wondered if it was too soon. She was remarkably quick to take in all he taught her. That morning she had managed the 'easy' killer Sudoku all by herself and was still glowing with pride in her own achievement. (Will had suggested a mark on the calendar to show she'd done the puzzle. She'd chosen a happy face and put it between his red tick – the vitamins – and the yellow cross whose significance she didn't know.) She'd learned the combinations of numbers (the only way to make three is with a one and a two; the only way to make seventeen is with a nine and an eight, and so on) very quickly, and had a firm grasp of the idea of establishing that a 'hanging out box' had to be whatever was over the forty-five that all the squares in a section had to add up to. Even on Fridays and Saturdays, when the puzzle was labelled 'deadly killer' and could take Will well over an hour to complete, she could usually find something she could put in – and did so with glee. Understanding the cryptic crossword was slower in coming, but it was coming, he was sure of that. He'd always hoped for intelligence and quick learning, but the joy she found it in all was an unexpected bonus.

But was she ready to take on the mantle, the task he had in mind for her? Would this be rushing her – and somehow spoil things in the end? Of course he wouldn't expect the impossible, she was still a little girl, after all, but she did show such promise. More, much more, promise than...

'What's my main present then?' she interrupted his reverie. He smiled again. Yes indeed, she was still only a little girl.

'Wait and see,' he said firmly but with what he hoped was a twinkle. 'But you can choose what cake you'd like now. We can make it together or we can go into Burton and buy one.' He knew she would choose the former and sure enough she did, spending an hour poring over the pictures and recipes, comparing the pros and cons of each, and finally agreeing to his suggestion that he surprise her, even though it meant their not doing it together.

'But that's all right,' she said, 'You can do it when I'm having my bath.'

•

'Does it seem funny to you that the police don't ask Milly and Jock to get on the telly and ask Jessie to come home?' Agnes had been puzzling over this for a few days. She had been rather looking forward to seeing her neighbours on the ten o'clock news; it would likely enhance her own status in the street. Who knows, maybe she and Les would get interviewed properly, or be asked to make an appeal for Jessie's freedom. When she couldn't sleep she rehearsed in her mind what she might say that would be the key to Jessie's discovery and release. How grateful the police – and Milly of course – would be then. She might even get a reward. She and Les could have a holiday abroad on it. Lanzarote or Magaluf, or maybe even some posh shopping in Paris.

'Well, no. Given that Jock keeps saying he'll paste the living daylights out of her when she comes home, I can't think the police would think it's a good idea for him to get up there and say "you're not in any trouble, we just want you home".' Les was quite pleased at the way the police seemed to be thinking along the same lines as he wanted them to where Jock was concerned. But now there was another player in the little drama – Jessie's real father had been located in Hexham and he had been on the telly, begging whoever took his much-loved little girl to let her go.

'Much loved? That's rich, coming from him!' Agnes felt no great affection for Howard, not least because he'd walked out on Milly thus leaving the field a bit clearer for her Les to go trespassing. 'He hasn't seen her since she was three years old or so. They may have got him on telly but he's a suspect an' all.' She didn't even attempt to hide her satisfaction at that, though privately she thought Jock was a more likely candidate if it had to be someone in the family. Personally she leaned towards the total stranger theory, the crazy sex perv, as she thought of him.

What didn't seem to strike any of them – Jock, Milly, Agnes or Les – was the almost complete absence of grieving and anxiety over the disappearance of the ten-year-old. Indeed, they seemed more concerned about a six-year-old boy who'd gone missing overnight in Bradford and were almost disappointed when he was found safe and sound the next morning, cuddled up to the dog on his granny's porch two streets away.

Any grieving that was being done in the shabby mid-terrace house that Jessie used to call home was done by David. He was visibly distressed, though none of the grownups in his daily life seemed to notice. He couldn't sleep, he wasn't eating properly and he wasn't concentrating in school. His teacher eventually noticed and sent a note home, asking if the boy was 'upset about his missing sister'. Jock responded in his usual brutal way so David struggled to keep his feelings to himself. When he did sleep he dreamed he'd found Jessie or that she'd come home with presents for him, and when he woke up, in a wet bed of course, he cried as silently as he could until it was time to get up and go to school. Even the police had no time for him now. They'd grilled him several times and got nowhere – because David knew nothing to tell them – and now seemed not to notice his existence.

He was also terrified that whoever had taken his sister would come back for him. And yet in a way he hoped they would. On balance he'd rather be with Jessie than left alone with Jock. He didn't count Milly; she might as well not be there anyway, she never stood up for him. Jessie was the only person in his life who had ever been on his side and that hadn't happened very often either. He tried harder to think of something that would help the police to find his sister. Officer Ferguson had told him that he must know something, even if he didn't know he knew it.

David couldn't think what it might be though.

EIGHT

He sat up, wide awake instantly, but shaking and sweating alarmingly.

'Only a dream,' he said out loud to reassure himself, 'breathe, breathe...' But such loud screaming; he could still hear it, and he couldn't be sure he wasn't still in the dream...

The ferry lurched madly and car alarms began shrieking from the vehicle deck. Will clung to his seat, and then noticed that other passengers were disregarding the ban on visiting the vehicle deck whilst the ferry was at sea. They were pouring through the door that led down to that deck. Had he closed the boot properly? Was it really locked? The idea of other people milling around his car, carrying its awful secret, drove him to leave the relative safety of his seat and struggle down the iron staircase to the lower deck.

People were everywhere – far more people than could possibly have got on board when he did. And the more he looked, the more people there seemed to be. He pushed through groups, desperately looking for his car. Was it in row F? Or row H? He couldn't find it and he couldn't remember where he'd parked it. He couldn't see any row signs with letters either; they all seemed to have numbers now.

He decided to start at one end and go down each row, but before he could begin he saw a huge crowd of people standing around a car that must be his. The boot was open and there was a dead girl inside. But she wasn't dead, she was screaming. Loud, piercing screams, that almost shattered his eardrums. 'STOP!' he yelled and lunged for the car.

He was awake but he could still hear the screaming. He shook himself. Oh God, it was Ariel!

Will shot out of bed, not stopping for his dressing gown, and was at her bedside before he'd even taken a second breath.

'Wake up Jessie, wake up. It's all right, it's only a dream.' He held the little body tightly, stroking her back and speaking soothingly to her as she began to calm down and wake up. 'That was a bad one eh?' he said when she seemed more alert. 'Want to tell me about it?'

She was silent but calmer. Will didn't know if it would be better to push her to talk or to let her go back to sleep – if she could. 'I'll make us a chocolate drink, then you can tell me if you like, or you can go safely back to sleep, knowing it was only a dream.'

He went downstairs to the kitchen, Jessie padding after him in her too-big hand-me-down pyjamas. He made the cocoa and they sat at the kitchen table to drink it. He decided not to press for answers, she would tell him if she wanted or needed to.

'I miss my mum,' she suddenly said, loudly, and burst into tears again. 'I want to go home. I don't want to go to Norwich, I want to go home.'

This was the last thing Will had expected. She hadn't mentioned Norwich for two weeks or more and she had never mentioned missing Sheringham. What could have brought this on? And what should he do? Delay – that had always worked in the past, and Will felt he had a PhD in delaying tactics by now.

'All right. If that's what you want.'

'It is, it IS,' she sobbed.

'All right but please calm down. We can't do anything tonight, it's half past three in the morning, but if you still want to go when it gets light, then you shall. I shall be disappointed, very disappointed, but I care too much about you to make you unhappy.'

She was quieter, though still sobbing softly.

'Have you forgotten it's your birthday tomorrow – well, today now? We were planning a celebration.'

She didn't answer and he felt slightly uncomfortable about using such emotional black-mail. But he would, if it came to that. There was no way he was giving her up now.

They finished their cocoa in silence and then he took her hand and led her back to bed. She got in, lay down, and immediately rolled on her side, turning her face away from him.

'Would you like me to stay until you fall asleep?' She didn't answer but he decided he would stay anyway. He knew there would be no more sleep for him that night so he might as well spend the time in here with Ariel as out there, pacing, planning, cursing. Damn. Had he made a mistake again? Had he rushed things? No, she had shown no sign of reluctance at any of his programme for her. Maybe he had just underestimated the pull of home and mother, even when a child is having a wonderful time and life at home hasn't been all that good. He remembered reading about a little boy whose mother had deliberately set him on fire, yet in hospital he had cried for his mother and could not, would not, be comforted by anyone else. He didn't know a great deal about Jessie's home life, but the little bits that had emerged left him feeling that it had been no place for a sensitive ten-year-old. Eleven-year-old now, it was already her birthday. What was he going to do about that?

'Can't cross a bridge till you come to it,' he reminded himself, and settled himself into the chair near her bed for the rest of the night.

•

'Today is Jessie Pike's eleventh birthday. Police looking for the little girl, missing since 1st February, say they are no closer to finding her than they have ever been. Every lead has turned into a blank and not one of the several hundred calls from the public has offered anything of substance. No clue, no trace of Jessie has been found, and intensive searches of her family home, her natural father's home, and 200 neighbourhood homes have revealed nothing.

'Police spokesman Peter Ferguson was joined by Jessie's mother, 28-year-old Milly Douglas, her stepfather, 36-year-old Jock Douglas, her natural father, 29-year-old Howard Pike, and Jessie's nine-year-old brother, David, at a press conference last night. The family did not speak, but Officer Ferguson stressed that Jessie was sorely missed and would not be in any trouble when she got home. He appealed to her kidnapper to put her back into a safe place, for his sake as well as hers.'

Another paragraph regurgitated in abbreviated form all that had been written about her before, finishing with a final appeal to anyone who knew anything at all to get in touch with their local police. Interestingly there was no longer a dedicated telephone number to ring.

Will scanned the item online quickly and shut it down. Nothing new, no clues. There wouldn't be, of course, unless she'd accidentally dropped an item of clothing or something, and that would have been found long ago. With all the CCTV cameras all over Britain it was a miracle she had totally escaped detection, but if anyone had seen her – or them – they would have come forward long before this. Of course, the police might have something up their sleeve, something they were keeping secret so as to tighten the net, but he couldn't seriously believe that. He felt fairly relaxed about it all. There was a pattern in the media attention given to these missing girls and this was moving along nicely.

No, that wasn't his problem this morning. Ariel's nightmare was what was causing him to feel anxious now. His own nightmare – meriting a black cross on the calendar, the first for six weeks – was just a faint memory now.

•

'What kind of cake have you made me?' They were at the breakfast table and to Jessie, Will seemed a bit quiet, especially as it was her birthday now. She'd expected a happy fuss right away, but he was hardly talking.

'Chocolate with butterscotch topping.' He smiled though, to her great relief.

'Oh yum! Can I see it? Can I have a piece now?' She looked at him and then, quickly, 'I mean may I?'

He patted her arm and grinned. 'Why not? It's your birthday after all. I think it's okay to do things differently on a birthday – within reason of course.'

He brought the cake to the table and cut them each a slice. 'Yummm, it's fab! You're a really good cake cooker.'

'Thank you.'

'Are we celebrating now, then?' Jessie was anxious to know what her main present was to be, and what else he had up his sleeve for her today. 'What are we going to do?'

He pulled his chair closer to her, turned to look her and said, 'First we need to clear something up. Do you remember having a nightmare last night and insisting that you want to go home?'

She did. And wished she didn't. 'Sort of.'

'Well I'd like to talk about that. I'm sure you miss your home, you must miss your mum and stepdad...'

'And David,' she interrupted.

'And David, yes. But remember when we met you wanted to go to Norwich to live with your dad, what happened to that?'

'Dunno.' She drooped. This wasn't going how she wanted it at all. She couldn't think what had possessed her to even say she wanted to go home – she didn't. And she no longer wanted to find her dad either, except it would be nice to show Will off to her family, she did have a fancy to do that some day.

'When you said that, it upset me. I had no idea, I thought we were getting along so well and that you were happy with me.'

'I am.' Oh dear, how could she get Nice Will back? 'I want to stay with you, I do.' She felt the tears pricking her eyes. What had she done? She was wrecking her birthday. 'Please. Ca... may I?'

'The thing is, if I take you back to Norfolk now I would get into terrible trouble. People would see it as kidnapping – they wouldn't believe that you had chosen to come with me. I'd go to jail you know. I don't think you'd like that, would you? I know I wouldn't.'

'Oh no,' the tears were flowing freely now. It was all ruined, her birthday, her life with Will. 'I don't want you to go to jail, Will. I couldn't bear that. I don't want to go back. I don't want to go to Norwich either. Please don't take me back there, I'll do anything... anything...'

'I don't know...'

'Oh please, Will, please, please, please.....'

He looked at her for a long moment. 'Well if you're sure...'

'I am! I want to stay with you. For ever.'

'You mustn't ever say it again then. We can put this one time behind us and carry on as we were, but if you say it again I shall have to believe that in your heart of hearts you want to go back to Sheringham.'

'I won't, I promise, I won't ever say it again. I won't even think it. I couldn't, because it isn't true. I don't know why I said it. Please, please, please, Will, let me stay with you?' Her tears were choking her and her nose was running. She didn't remember ever feeling so desperate.

'All right. We'll put it behind us then. Here, wipe your nose and dry your tears and let's have another piece of cake to celebrate getting over this nasty bit. Then we'll do something ordinary to draw a line under it, and then we'll get on with celebrating your eleventh birthday. Okay?'

'Okay, yes please.' She felt the relief flood through her whole body. She wanted to hug him. Would he object?

As so often happened, he was thinking the same thing. 'Shall we shake hands to seal the deal – or shall we have a hug?'

'A hug please,' and for the first time since they'd met, they hugged.

•

All in all, Will thought, it had gone pretty well. He felt a bit of a heel but so much was at stake. He couldn't afford to go through this again. Waiting for her to come down for breakfast he had felt more anxious than he had for what seemed like ages. Even counting cars as they passed—two-to-one to Whittington; two-all; three-two from Whittington—usually a reliably calming activity, had done little to soothe his ragged nerves. Thinking about how he would teach Ariel to use this technique to combat any anxiety helped a little, but not as much as he needed.

But he'd enjoyed the hug. To his surprise and delight, he'd felt a slight stirring and although he knew he would never do anything about it with her – not for a few years anyway – he was pleased to discover he wasn't dead yet. Not in that department.

Had he felt aroused by the others? He'd expected to, but couldn't remember if, in fact, he had been particularly. But they'd been fifteen – that would have been a normal reaction;

Ariel was only just eleven. Had she reached puberty yet? He didn't think so, he would have known, surely, if she'd had a period. A thought struck him; did she know about such things? At what age does a mother tell her daughter what to expect? He had no idea. He had no sisters, no brothers either for that matter; his knowledge of girls was severely limited.

He thought there was a small supply of sanitary pads in one of the boxes in Ariel's cupboard. He'd kept everything the other girls had ever owned. He liked to think it was with an eye on the future; it would all come in handy.

Perhaps he'd look on the web to see what sort of age girls started menstruating. Maybe he could even find something about how to tell them what it was all about – if they didn't already know. Perhaps Jessie's mother had always been open about these things, or perhaps she'd picked up information from school friends. But at least he had a plan for now. Thank the lord for the internet. He'd get the information and take it from there. 'Another bridge to cross when I come to it,' he reassured himself. Meanwhile there was a birthday to celebrate. Her last – on the fifth of March, anyway.

NINE

Jessie had mixed feelings about the success of her birthday. It had started very badly.

When she'd come into the kitchen that morning she had been startled to see Will standing at the window, muttering numbers to himself as an occasional car passed. He'd stopped as soon as he saw her, so she hadn't commented. And although they had agreed to draw a line under it, she was still shaken by her dream. She couldn't actually remember what the dream had been about, but she knew she'd upset Will by saying she wanted to go back to Sheringham. She didn't want to go home and she didn't really want to go to Norwich any more, but she was missing David something terrible. She wondered if there was any way David might be able to come and visit, or better still, come and live with them. Her innate sense of timing told her not to mention that today, so she settled into the business of celebrating her eleventh birthday.

Will gave her several presents including some books she didn't think she was going to like right away, but if he thought they were good, then she was willing to give them a go. Until Will, she hadn't exactly read for pleasure but reading was important to Will so it was important to her now. A Christmas Carol looked the most promising so she got started on it that afternoon. So far, so good ; Tiny Tim was quite sweet, she thought, and she liked the way people took tender care of him. Will also gave her a necklace: a piece of shiny pink stone hanging on what looked like a shoelace. She had a hunch it wasn't new, but it didn't matter; Will had give it to her. She would wear it for ever, always. Best of all he gave her a pair of binoculars for their birding walks. Up to now she'd borrowed a pair of his, but they'd driven into Birmingham after their birthday cake breakfast, where he'd bought her a smaller pair, a pair she could handle more easily. Their celebration had been to go out on one of their favourite walks so she could try them out, packing themselves large slices of the chocolate-butterscotch cake. They had identified a willow tit (she could tell right away that it wasn't a coal tit or a blue tit or a great tit) and to her great joy Will had said 'It's your birthday bird!' and she'd carefully, in her very best handwriting, written down 'Will-Oh tit' on her Life List.

But the binoculars apparently hadn't been her 'main' present. Will seemed to have changed his mind about that and she couldn't help feeling that had something to do with her dream and middle-of-the-night scene about going home. Yet he didn't seem in the least bit angry with her.

'Birthdays are fun, aren't they?' he said, as they were having their supper – spaghetti bol, chosen by her. 'And you know what,' he paused, 'you are going to have another birthday very soon.'

She was gobsmacked. 'What do you mean?'

'Your next birthday is going to be on the tenth of May and from now on that's when we're going to celebrate you.'

'Will I be eleven again then, or will I be twelve?' This sort of thing was important to Jessie.

'Hmmm, eleven, I should think. It's only two months and five days away, so you can't really be twelve. Will you mind being eleven for two extra months?'

She didn't think so. And certainly the idea of another birthday so soon was very appealing. But she did wonder, 'Why am I having another birthday?'

He got his 'special face' on and said solemnly: 'The tenth of May is a very special day and that needs to be your birthday from now on. And on that day I shall give you a very special present, the present I had thought to give you today, but in thinking about it further I realise it has to be given to you on the tenth of May.' He smiled. 'So contain your soul in patience and enjoy today.'

She thought that wouldn't be too hard. Two months and five days would go pretty quickly. A thought struck her. 'When's your birthday, Will?'

'I celebrate my birthday on the fifth of November, another very special day.'

'Yes!' she was excited, 'It's Bonfire Night! Lucky!'

'So it is,' he seemed not to have noticed. 'But it has another significance which I shall tell you about on the tenth of May. Now – bath time!'

•

The police activity had begun to lessen. From hundreds of personnel working on the case, the number was down to one dedicated part-time officer. No one was actively searching for Jessie any more, and no more houses or trash bins were being gone through with a fine-tooth comb. Jock, Milly and David were able to move back into their own home – much to the relief of both Agnes and Les. Agnes was relieved not to be washing wet sheets every day or so, but most of her relief was because she didn't like having Milly sleeping under the same roof as her Les. Les didn't either – it gave him all sorts of hard-to-deal-with feelings in regions of his body that he was not accustomed to thinking about so much.

David was glad to be home. If he was going to wake up in a wet bed he wanted it to be his own wet bed. But curiously, he stopped doing it from the very first night he got back. Milly had told him he could have Jessie's room if he wanted – just let her clear out all Jessie's stuff when she got round to it. He wasn't sure at first. It was certainly a better room than his little box cupboard, but it seemed a bit too soon to assume she was never coming back. He'd overheard Agnes offering to help Milly load all Jessie's clothes into black plastic bin bags and drop them off at Barnardo's. 'Won't she want them when she comes back?' he'd asked.

'She'll probably have grown out of them anyway,' said Agnes. 'She'll be wanting summat new in any case, if I know eleven-year-olds.'

That's right, he thought, she's eleven now. And she was ten when she went missing, so she's been gone for a whole year. 'They're quite likely right then,' he told himself, pleased with his maths, 'she won't be coming back.'

After that he stopped thinking about her so much, and got on with the business of planning his move to her old room. For some reason he seemed to be getting on better with Jock, too, so life was looking up for David Pike. And it wasn't long till his birthday, either. The Angel twins had told him that now that he was an only child he'd get better presents – his mum could spend the money she hadn't spent on Jessie for her birthday on him. That happy thought got him off to sleep every night with no trouble at all.

•

Of all the new activities Will had brought into Jessie's life, identifying and listing birds was far and away her favourite. She looked over her Life List almost daily, comparing it with her British Birds book, and asking Will where – and when – she might see this or that bird. She examined his Life List and asked how soon she would be getting close to his life number. It was a very rare day that she didn't spend some time outside with her binoculars, scouring the hedgerows for signs of activity, always looking for something she had not yet identified and ticked on her list. She had over 30 already and she'd only been doing it for, what, three months? Will had told her she had almost certainly seen many, many more but had not identified them. She might, then, be nearly up to his Life List.

Will didn't like her to be outside without him, though she couldn't fathom why. Nobody ever came down their track, not even the postman; he deposited Will's scanty post in a locked wooden box at the top of the drive where it met the winding back road that would, eventually, lead into the village. They hardly ever went into the village, though they often drove through on their way to Lichfield or Birmingham. When Burton was on the agenda they would turn left out of the driveway and miss Whittington entirely. Will seemed to prefer going left; it was safer, he said. Turning right to get on to the correct side of the road involved crossing blind, because of the slight hill and sharp corners to their left. There wasn't a lot of traffic on their road, but what there was tended to go rattling past at an alarming speed.

'What's your favourite thing to do, Will?' she asked him one morning.

'Hmmm, I'm not sure I have a favourite.' He was reading but put the book down to consider. 'Anything that has to do with learning, I suppose. I like learning new things. I like the challenge of getting to know something I don't already know and like. And I like teaching what I know – which isn't really all

47

that much – to others, particularly to you.'

'Who else do you teach to?'

'There hasn't been anybody for a long time,' he smiled at her, 'That's why I'm so happy to have you here.'

Jessie was certainly happy to be there. Her bad dream, evoking homesickness, had not returned and she found herself thinking less and less of David – who had been, briefly, the only one she'd given any real thought to, her dad being a very shadowy figure. She did sometimes indulge in a fantasy of showing off her new life, taking Will to Sheringham and flaunting him. David would be impressed, so would the Angel twins. And her mother and Jock would be sorry they'd treated her so badly. They'd beg her to come back and she'd be kind but firm in her refusal. Eventually Jock would threaten her and then Will would come to her rescue, looming over the stunted Jock, and saying something like, 'She's with me now.' And he'd help her into his car and they'd drive away, her waving in a dignified but sorrowful way at the weeping family as they tried to cling on to the car. Then in the car Will would say 'Don't you worry. You're mine now, I'll take care of you for ever.'

Another fantasy, when that one palled for a while, was showing him off to her dad. Will was far better as a dad to her than ever her real dad had been; she'd like the chance to say that. The scene she imagined with Jock and her mum would probably work just as well with her dad, she thought.

'Did you teach your cousin? Before she died?' Jessie wanted to know more about Will and more about his family. He didn't seem to have any family – or friends. That struck Jessie as odd; in her old house somebody was always coming in or out, having a cup of tea, or coming to stop overnight on the lumpy sofa in the lounge.

'Yes. That is, I tried, but she wasn't a good learner. She didn't catch on to things like you do and she wasn't really interested. I was actually quite glad when she... when she stopped coming.'

'How old was she?'

'Oh, about fifteen I think. She was older than you but not

much bigger. Maybe she was fourteen or even thirteen. I don't remember really.'

Jessie could tell he didn't want to talk about the mysterious cousin, but she was very curious. Will's reluctance to talk only made her more curious. 'What did she die of?'

'Jessie, I really don't want to talk about her. Can we just drop it? She isn't here any more and I don't think about her at all, so please, let's just leave her alone.' For the first time in their relationship he was short with her.

She was horrified by this. 'Yes, yes. I'm sorry, Will. I won't ask about her any more, I promise.'

He seemed to recover immediately and smiled at her. 'Good girl. Shall we have a hug on that?'

•

Had Ariel-II been so curious about Ariel-I? He didn't think so. In fact, A-II hadn't been curious about anything much at all. That had been part of the problem and why, sadly and reluctantly, he'd had to admit defeat and remove her, as he'd had to do with A-I, for that matter. He'd picked a couple of duds, but not this time. This time he knew he'd got the right one. So much so, in fact, that he wasn't even thinking of her as Ariel-III, but simply as Ariel. The first. The best. No, the only.

And it was only a matter of days before he was to bestow the Ariel mantle on Jessie. He would quite like it to be a ceremony, but what? What had he done with the others? Nothing, really; maybe that had been part of the problem. He'd simply told them right at the beginning that as far as he was concerned their name was Ariel and they'd seemed to go along with it. Or maybe they'd just ignored it. Of course, they'd been older than Jessie. It hadn't occurred to him before that a better way to get a suitable fifteen-year-old Ariel was to start with a ten- or eleven-year-old and bring her on. What a stroke of luck that he had seen Jessie on that February evening – running away as the original Ariel had actually considered doing – and that she'd been so willing to join him in his quest. Well, she hadn't really, he knew that, but it wasn't hard for him now to block out her early hesitation and see her, from the beginning, as an eager and willing participant in his fantasy; their future life together as Will and Ariel Dee.

She certainly was willing now, even though she wasn't aware of the full extent of his plan for their future. For the umpteenth time he wondered how much he should tell her on the tenth. Certainly he should explain about the original Will and Ariel and his hope that the two of them together would continue their work. Perhaps that should be all for the time being; let the rest evolve in its appropriate time. You can't tell an eleven-year-old that she's going to marry a thirty-something when she's fourteen. Mind you, not much more than a hundred years ago thirteen had been the legal age of consent. And in some Eastern countries girls got married at eight. How he wished he'd met his Ariel at eight.

TEN

On the eighth of May Will gave Jessie a small suitcase and instructed her to pack enough clothes for a two-night stay away. They were going to London. They were going to the theatre in the afternoon and they were going out to a very posh restaurant for an early supper. And before that they were going to buy Jessie the appropriate clothes, in London, for their outing.

Listening to the plan, Jessie was beside herself with excitement. All these wonderful things and still Will said, 'No, that's not your main present either.' What could that be? She couldn't imagine but she knew it would be something wonderful.

What she didn't know though, was how to pack a suitcase. Will had to help her, teaching her gently as always. 'First put the bigger items in as flat as they'll go, then put a layer of tissue paper between them... roll up your socks and underwear and tuck them round the sides... finish with your toilet articles in the lid compartment, and any other odds and ends you might need. And don't forget to pack a book to read as well as your journal. And a pen, of course, you can't do much with your journal if you don't have a pen.'

Will had introduced her to the idea of journaling her thoughts and feelings, as well as her activities, two weeks ago. He'd smiled at her descriptions of what they did each day: 'brill', 'awesome, 'great' or 'cool', and told her the next item on their agenda was for her to learn some more descriptive words. He said they'd spend some time on their car journey to London finding some new-to-her words to describe what she was feeling and seeing; adjectives and adverbs, they were called. 'Brill,' she'd said, cheekily, and hugged him hard. She couldn't imagine being any happier, and told him so. He was happy too; she knew that. His nice brown eyes twinkled a lot and he was often to be heard humming or whistling as he went about his day.

He reminded her at teatime that if the subject came up, she was his niece, visiting for a few days. She hadn't liked that. It nearly spoiled her excitement about their outing. Couldn't he be her dad? Even though she called him Will? She could tell he wasn't keen and she felt disappointed. She thought she'd write about that in her journal and use the word 'sad'. It certainly wasn't awesome.

But he didn't say no, so with years of experience at knowing when you've got your way and it's time to shut up, she said no more. She just hugged the idea to herself that he was now her dad and that they were going to London tomorrow to celebrate her special birthday. It would have been nice if he'd been as keen as she was on the new arrangement, but in truth she didn't really need it to complete her sense of utter happiness. In any case, she'd thought of him as her dad for some time now, even if he didn't know it. She did risk one parting shot though as she left the room to have her bath.

'Dads are much more special than uncles.'

•

Dad! He was aghast. He didn't want to be her dad; he wasn't her dad. Damn! How could she have got it so wrong? How could he have got it so wrong? And more to the point, what could he do about it so that it didn't spoil tomorrow? He should have been much firmer in the past. Now he was facing the second damn birthday in a row that had been spoiled by the difference between what she wanted and what he was determined to have. He hoped this wasn't going to become a habit.

Will paced up and down the lounge, keeping his ear open for sounds that she had finished her bath and was waiting for him to go in to say goodnight. He couldn't let her see how upset he was. But tonight! The night before his big declaration, the Big Reveal, tonight of all nights, for her to spring that on him. How had he not seen that coming? He wanted to cry with frustration and disappointment. Hell! He was crying.

'Music,' he said out loud, blowing his nose and wiping his eyes, 'Music is what I need to calm me down. This won't do.' He picked up a CD – just about any CD from his collection would do – it turned out to be Berwald's Sinfonie Capricieuse. A good choice: the sheer exuberance of the opening Allegro followed quickly by the principal theme and then the distinctly capricious secondary theme restored his equilibrium quickly. As did remembering that this soul-stirring piece had itself been the subject of considerable controversy and the revision of the original score – which had been lost – seemed to him to be an omen. 'Best laid plans,' he muttered and, catching sight of himself in the mirror above the fireplace, he grimaced. 'All right. It's not the end of the world. Say nothing. And above all, don't let her see how upset you are about it and maybe it will die down.' After all, he hadn't been going to reveal his ultimate plan to her tomorrow. Really nothing was lost. So, taking a lesson from Berwald, maybe a revised score will be better even than the original.

He smiled at his reflection. A bit tight-lipped still, a rictus smile, but a smile nevertheless. 'Brill,' he said acidly to the mirror, and went to say goodnight to Ariel.

•

They set off early on the morning of the ninth, turning left out of the driveway to avoid a heart-stopping dash to the other side; then, because Jessie always enjoyed and admired his prowess, and because he enjoyed her admiration, doing a perfect three-point turn in the road where the view was clearer. They'd packed an egg sandwich for Jessie because she'd been too excited to eat her breakfast. What a difference, she thought, her mother probably wouldn't even have noticed – or she'd have ganged up with Jock to tell her she'd eat it or else. Will had simply said 'never mind, we'll take something with us and you can eat it in the car when you're hungry'. What a dad! But she didn't say that. Jessie hadn't spent all those years under Jock's regime without learning how to keep quiet when it was important.

The journey down the M1 was thrilling to Jessie, who had never been further than Cromer in her waking hours (you couldn't count the drive to Will's house because she'd been asleep). She was enthralled with the idea that you go up to London, even as you're going down the motorway, and kept saying: 'We're going up to London, down the M1.' Will had decided not to show her their route on a map in case she'd asked where Norwich is, but he decided to risk broadening her horizons a bit further by telling her that if they took the ferry to mainland Europe they'd be going across to Paris, but once they got on to French soil, they'd be going up to Paris, even though they were heading south. He thought if she asked what they would be doing if they went to Norwich he would be able to handle it. But she didn't, and every time she admired something, or exclaimed in delight, Will helped her find a new word to better describe her feelings. Like everything else with Will, that was fun. 'Absolutely fantastic fun,' she said and earned another pat on the shoulder.

Between learning new words, they worked on the day's crossword, in itself a reliable source of good new words. Will had stopped in Whittington on their way through and bought The Times for them to have on the journey. Sometimes she caught on immediately when Will explained the crossword answer and how he'd arrived at it, more often she didn't. Puns were especially hard to see, although she usually sort of understood it after Will told her the answer. Butter may be seen here enjoying continuing success turned out to be 'on a roll'. She thought that over for a long time, wondering how Will had worked it out even as she thought she saw that it was the right answer.

'It will come,' he said. 'You have to get in the habit of thinking differently, that's all. Remember the joke you told me the other day? When is a door not a door?'

'When it's ajar.' She was on safer ground here.

'Right, that's a kind of pun. A door can be ajar – slightly open – but it can't be a door if it's a jar. A good crossword clue for that, by the way, would be 'open container' – the jar being the container and ajar meaning open. With me?'

'Yes,' sort of, she thought to herself.

'Another good one, for the word late, would be dead on time, not really. When people are dead they are referred to as 'late' – the late Mrs Beeton, for example – and you know what late means in terms of time. So if you're dead (late) you aren't on time, are you?'

She shook her head, bemused. She'd almost kept up with him, till the 'late' clue, but she had hope, and knew Will would keep helping her. Much later she remembered how nearly she'd said 'like the late Cousin Sally', and was pleased with herself that she'd somehow had the sense not to.

'It will come,' he said again. 'Meanwhile, let's talk about anagrams; they're more easy to spot.'

'What's anagrams?' Jessie wondered just how many new words she was going to have to learn that day. Journaling was going to take some time tonight.

'Ah. First of all it would be what are anagrams, not what is.'

She got that, and nodded.

'An anagram is when you take the letters – all the letters – in a word or phrase and rearrange them – all of them – into another word or phrase. Lime, for example, L-I-M-E, can be rearranged to make mile: M-I-L-E. And lemon – the letters in lemon can be rearranged to make melon. It's actually what we do on Countdown, in the final round, and up to a point, in the polygon. Yes?'

'Yes,' she nodded enthusiastically, willing to believe.

'Well, with anagram clues there's always a word that tells you that you need to rearrange the letters of one or more of the other words. Here's one, for example,' he glanced quickly at the paper and then back to the road. 'Linen – all of it needs sorting out, to be conventional. When I see the words "needs sorting out", I feel fairly sure that's an anagram. It's telling me to "sort out" some letters. Then I look for a word or a combination of words that add up to the number of letters I need for the answer. In this case, it's "linen, all of it" because the answer to the clue is three words, each four letters long, and "linen, all of it" is twelve letters. And three fours are twelve, as you know.' He looked over at her. 'With me so far?'

'I think so,' she said, not sure at all that she was, but keen to continue. She wanted to get it because she knew he would be pleased with her when she did. Besides, Will talking to her about anything was magic, she thought. No one had ever talked to her about things before. She liked it. She liked it a lot.

'Right, so you rearrange all those letters in "linen, all of it" and you're looking for a phrase that means to be conventional. The definition – what the clue answer means – is always either the first part of the clue or the last. You don't get told which though, you have to work it out, sometimes you have to guess.'

'What does conventional mean?' Jessie was really struggling hard now.

'Oh, pretty much doing what everyone else is doing, normal, ordinary, not standing out as different. Not like us! We aren't conventional. We don't 'fall-into-line' – would you know what I meant if I said that?'

She wasn't sure but hazarded a guess. 'Is that the answer then – fall into line?'

'Yes! Well done. Put that in five down and later we'll look at the clues across that use those letters. But that's enough schooling on that subject for now, I think.'

School. Jessie didn't really want to bring up the subject – she always liked to know where a touchy subject was going before she introduced it – but on the other hand, while everything was going so well, now might be a good time. 'Will I have to go back to school soon?' She held her breath.

'Do you want to?' Will kept driving steadily, his eyes on the road.

'Not really. I like learning with you.'

'Then why go to school? I certainly like teaching you although I'm sure there are things you'd learn about in school that I either don't think of or I don't know enough about. But if you're happy with the way things are, then let's keep them that way. It's easier. If we enrolled you in the Whittington school, for example, we'd have to explain who you are and that might be difficult. We'd have to lie or they'd take you back to Sheringham. It might even end up with my being arrested for snatching you and ending up in jail.'

'No you wouldn't! You didn't snatch me. I wanted to come with you and I'd tell them that. And I'd tell them that I want to stay with you so they couldn't arrest you.'

'It doesn't actually work like that, but I'm really happy you're happy. That makes me even happier. So no more talk about school, eh? Agreed?'

'Agreed.' She patted his arm. 'And when we stop we'll have a hug to seal it.' She liked this new habit. He was a good hugger. He was a good everything, really. Why in the world would she want to go to school when she could spend all her time with Will? She didn't miss children of her own age. She'd had no special friends at Sheringham school; she'd hung around with Gabriel and Michael sometimes but having a Best Friend had not been possible because she wouldn't have wanted to bring them home. She'd played in the street with whoever else was out and about, but until Will she hadn't really had any concept of what it could be like to have a soul mate. She and Will played card games and board games and often they had a giggle together. They talked about serious things and they talked about silly things. There was nothing she could get at school that she wasn't getting more of, and better, at home with Will. She tucked into her egg sandwich and settled down to contemplate what sort of outfit she might get for tomorrow's theatre and dinner.

•

Will had deliberately chosen a large anonymous and impersonal hotel near the West End. He'd thought long and hard about it, but had finally opted for adjoining rooms. He must stay aware of his tendency to rush things. This was going so well; he must not do anything to jeopardize its success.

He felt nervous as they checked in as Will Dee and Miss A Dee, but nobody seemed to be paying him any undue attention. He declined assistance with the suitcases and he and Jessie got into the lift and up to the fifth floor to find their rooms. Jessie was enchanted – as he'd known she would be. She couldn't decide whether to look out of the window, to bounce on the beds, or to examine the toiletries in the bathrooms. 'Oh look! There's a television in your bathroom! And a phone! Is there one in mine? YES! I can watch television in the bath and phone somebody. I think I'll phone you.' She ran back and forth, exulting and exclaiming until Will thought he'd better try to calm her down – at least a little.

'How about unpacking – putting your things into the drawers – and then we can go out and get some lunch before we do The Big Shop?'

That did the trick. She placed her few clothes lovingly into the drawers and put her suitcase away in the cupboard. 'I'm ready. And I'm hungry – it was a good egg sandwich, Will, but it didn't stay with me very long.'

Even so, when they found a suitable place for a quick lunch she wasn't able to eat much. 'I'm too excited about shopping for my tomorrow-outfit.'

'I know you are, but you're going to need the strength to get through all that looking and trying on.' He was thoroughly enjoying watching her and experiencing her pleasure in it all. Her enthusiasm reminded him that a visit to London could actually be a magical event.

'See if you can manage a few more mouthfuls, but if you really can't, don't worry. We'll have a break and have afternoon tea at the Ritz. You can indulge your sweet tooth in scones and cream and trifle. Not to mention cucumber sandwiches and petits fours.

'What's petty four please?' She switched quickly into learning mode, as he'd known she would, and ate a little more of her lunch as he explained why so many English cakes have French names.

Will had a quick coffee, mindful of her impatience to get moving! And they were off to Oxford Street. He had no real idea which shops would be suitable, but it didn't matter. She was rapidly in and out of several – 'no, nothing there' – until they found Next. It wouldn't have been his choice but she was delighted and in no time at all found not one but two dresses that she declared were 'to die for'.

'Well, I wouldn't want that, so we'd better get them both. Maybe you can decide over tea which you'd like to wear tomorrow.'

'I've already decided. I'm going to wear the blue one for the theatre and the yellow one with flowers for the dinner.' From the look on her face Will could see there was no point in even discussing it. Not that he minded; he thought she looked the bee's knees in both – and told her so, much to her delight.

'The bee's knees? I think I look better than that. I think I look like a film star's knees.' They both giggled and Will thought he'd never been happier in his entire life. And the big moment hadn't even been reached yet.

They had tea at the Ritz, though in truth Jessie was really too tired to make the most of it. She'd wanted to use the underground to get back to the hotel – she declared herself 'in love' with the escalators – but Will knew from experience that she was reaching exhaustion point and needed a soothing bath and bed very soon.

'Tomorrow,' he said. 'Tomorrow is your special day, so if you want to spend it all riding escalators and the underground, then so you shall. But tonight I must make sure you have a good night's rest, so we're having a taxi.'

She leaned against him in the taxi, nearly asleep, but just awake enough to tell him she felt well happy with life. Unable to resist an opportunity to improve her vocabulary, he responded: 'Content. That's what you're feeling: content. Me too.'

She had a quick bath, turning down his offer to put on her television, and was in bed and asleep before they had been back in the hotel for 45 minutes. Will closed the connecting door and rang room service for his dinner. It wasn't long before he, too, was in and out of the bath and into bed and contentedly asleep.

ELEVEN

'Once upon a time,' Will began, after they'd had breakfast and were back in their rooms, 'there was a man named Will Durant. He was a teacher in America, a very good teacher, who loved learning and loved passing on what he knew.'

'Like you,' Jessie said, already enjoying the story.

'Yes, very like me. And that's the point. His partner in learning and the woman he later married, was named Ariel, like you.'

'I'm not named Ariel.' Jessie was confused.

'Well, yes, you are now. To me, you've always been Ariel, but as from today – which is Ariel Durant's birthday, you are going to be Ariel. My Ariel, Ariel Dee, and we are going to learn things together, like we do now, only more so. And we are going to continue the Durants' work together. That is your main birthday present I've been waiting so long to give you. How does it feel, my Ariel?'

How did it feel? Jessie didn't know. She was aware of a sharp disappointment that a name was all she was getting, but on the other hand, Will was so happy and so serious about it, it must be important to him. Therefore it would be important to her. She certainly liked the idea of their working together on whatever it was – she knew Will would help her do whatever she was supposed to do and that was always nice. She searched her memory for one of the new words she'd learned yesterday. 'Splendid,' she said and smiled happily at him, 'I think it's splendid.'

He reached over and pulled her close to him. 'This is the most meaningful hug in our relationship,' he said, and she could have sworn he had tears in his eyes.

She thought about the name. Ariel. It sounded quite nice, but not like any name she'd heard before, except, she thought, a washing powder. And she was to be Ariel Dee – just like she would be if she was his daughter. That was a splendid thought all by itself. Dee was a much nicer name than Pike, too.

She remembered something. 'Did you change your name to Will because of him then? Is he the man you said you admired?'

'Well remembered! Yes, I did and he was. I didn't like my own name and I wanted to be as much like Will Durant as I could. That's why I've chosen the fifth of November to celebrate my birthday – it was his birthday. And of course the tenth of May was Ariel Durant's birthday; that's why we're celebrating you on this day from now on.

She didn't mind that. But, 'What was your name before then?'

He shook his head. 'I've forgotten. Deliberately. I so disliked it that I've pushed it out of my mind completely.'

'You haven't! You couldn't forget your name.' She looked disbelievingly at him.

'I promise you I have. You can choose to forget things you no longer want to think about. People do it all the time.'

That was an interesting thought. She pondered what she might like to deliberately forget but couldn't come up with anything immediately.

'I can't remember what I want to forget,' she giggled, but it didn't matter; she was more interested in getting on with the day anyway. She hoped she wasn't rushing Will through what was obviously an important moment for him, but she couldn't wait.

'What are we going to do this morning?'

'We have a choice,' he seemed fine about the change of subject. 'We could go to an art gallery and look at some famous paintings that I like, or we could go to the British Museum and look at any number of interesting things. Really old things. But to be fair, a place like that deserves a whole day or more. It would be hard to just drop in for an hour or two.'

'Well, we'll see the famous paintings then.' That was an easy decision. 'Can we go on the underground?'

'We can and we may. Keep them straight, Ariel. Grammar is very important in our line of work.' He ruffled her hair, but she already knew he wasn't upset with her. He was too happy about changing her name to Ariel, she could tell.

•

Will couldn't remember ever being as happy as he'd felt today. It was even better than yesterday, he thought. Her reaction had been more, really, than he could ever have expected. He'd woken up at four a.m. and suddenly realised that he'd been building up this 'main present' business for so long that whatever it turned out to be it would be an anticlimax for her. And seriously, he asked himself, it is likely that an eleven-year-old is going to be thrilled about having to change who she is and how she thinks of herself? Maybe he should have just introduced it gradually, calling her Ariel more and more, without making such a production of it. But it was too late now, she was expecting something magnificent (another of yesterday's words) so he'd better make sure she understood just how magnificent it was. In the event, he thought 'splendid' was a very good response and he'd had a hard time not crying when they hugged.

They spent a happy morning at the Courtauld Institute, though she didn't seem to enjoy the Impressionists as much as he did, nor as much as he would have liked her to. She seemed drawn more towards the realism of the floral still lifes and the gory hunting and fighting scenes. But never mind, appreciation of art was something else he would be teaching her. Perhaps they'd start with the Tate Modern so he could show her what wasn't art. At least in his opinion. He would be fair, he'd explain that different people had different tastes. He might not like certain genres (another new word to teach her) but that didn't mean those who did were wrong, he'd tell her, and knew she would side with him.

After a quick lunch they took the tube for one stop (he would have walked, but he knew—and treasured—how much she enjoyed the underground) to the theatre. He had wanted to take her to see The Importance of Being Earnest, but had not been able to get matinee tickets, so had settled on The Mikado instead. A good choice – with her usual acuity she caught on to the story immediately, and relished the antics of Ko-Ko and his ugly bride-to-be, Katisha. They'd stopped in Hatchards on their way back to the hotel to change for dinner and he bought her a CD of The Mikado because she knew it, and one of The Pirates of Penzance because he thought she would enjoy that, too. They also looked at some art books and he showed her how Monet had painted the same cathedral many times, to show how it could appear different at different times of the day. That got her attention and he realised it was going to be easier than he'd thought to move her out of realism – 'chocolate box' paintings, as he thought of them – into appreciating what he appreciated. He was a good teacher; he allowed himself to think that. He found ways to introduce even the most troublesome subjects in ways to interest an eleven-year-old He'd like to take her to Paris and show her the original Impression: Sunrise in the Musée d'Orsay, but that wouldn't be possible. She'd need a passport to travel abroad; how could he get that?

Dinner had been a tremendous success. The waiter had pulled out all the stops and pretended he thought Ariel was Will's date for the evening. 'Would madam care for some ice cream with that?' he'd asked in his best Uriah Heep manner. She'd giggled, but managed to say 'Madam would. Please,' and the two of them had giggled over it all the way back to the hotel.

'Would madam care for a bath before her bed?' Will had asked, and 'Madam would not, thank you,' she'd responded. 'Madam would just care to get into bed dirty tonight. It's madam's special birthday so she can do that.'

'What the hell?' he thought, 'we're going home tomorrow so they'll change the sheets anyway. Come to think of it, I shall do the same.'

•

They spent most of the journey back to Whittington Moor talking about the Durants. Well, Will talked, and she listened. Most of what Will told her went right over her head. To start with, she didn't have a clear idea of what a philosopher was. Nor could she really get her head round what civilization meant. Not the way Will talked about it, anyway. This might have made her anxious, but not with Will. She knew he would help her understand and with infinite patience. He said she was well on her way already, because she had such a good sense of humour.

'Humour,' Will told her, 'according to Will Durant, is based on perspective, which is the secret of philosophy.' She had no idea what he could possibly mean but she gathered that he seemed to think she had a good sense of humour and she liked that.

The bit she liked best was the story of their love, how they'd met when he was a teacher and she was a pupil at his school, and how he'd had to leave his job so he could marry her.

'Why? Why did he have to leave? He wasn't doing anything wrong, was he?'

'No, not really, but he was quite a bit older than Ariel. She was only fourteen, so people, especially in those days, thought it not quite nice, I suppose. I don't see anything wrong with it, do you?'

'No. Not if he was nice to her and not all schoolteachery like some teachers are. If he was more like you I think it would be all right. Though she could have just been like his daughter, like I am to you.' She held her breath, waiting for his response, hoping he wouldn't be too irritated with her.

'Well, for the moment. Perhaps that will change when you get older.'

'P'raps,' she responded, not really wanting it to, nor able to imagine how it might. But she was aware that he hadn't liked what she'd said, and had replied through rather tight lips, so she rapidly changed the subject. 'Did they have any children?'

'Yes, they had a daughter named Ethel.'

'Crikey! What an awful name. I'm glad you didn't change my name to Ethel.' She laughed.

'Me too, but I thought we might get a cat and call it Ethel. Would you like that?

'A cat! Oh yes please Will, I'd love that. When can we get it?'

'Soon. I expect there are plenty of kittens up for a home at this time of year. We'll look on the post office notice board in the village and see. Maybe we should get two. The Durants later adopted a little boy, too, and called him Louis. We could call them Ethel and Louis.'

She shook her head. 'Weird. Wee-udd. But okay. If we're

going to be like that Will and Ariel, we'll have to have an Ethel and a Louis.' She giggled. 'Poor little kittens.'

TWELVE

No green tick this morning, but a huge black cross on the calendar, angrily scratched on. It had been a particularly bad dream this time, taking him some considerable time to become fully awake and realise it was only a dream; that Ariel was not, in fact, dead in the boot of his car. It was all the worse because in this dream the girl had been this Ariel. That was a first. And doubly upsetting because he had absolutely no doubt that she would not end up dead in the boot of his car like the other two. So why had he dreamed she was? He knew, from his previous reading about dream interpretation on the internet, that Freudians believe all dreams contain a wish and a fear and often they are one and the same. But it was madness to think he either wished or feared this. Wasn't it?

He'd got up and made himself a cup of strong coffee and struggled to convince himself that this, too, was something he could choose to forget forever. But how? There was no traffic at that hour for him to count, so he got The Times online and scoured it for references to missing Jessie Pike. Nothing. Just to be sure, he Googled her name. He was doing that less and less, and these days there were fewer small black circles on the calendar to indicate a hit. Not a thing there either, unsurprisingly. The police had nothing to go on, no leads to follow up, no idea of where, even, to look any more. Given that the vast majority of missing children (something like 70,000 a year apparently) turned up safe and sound within four days, and most of them had never left their immediate area, there was nothing to bring police attention to the outskirts of a sleepy little village like Whittington – more than 100 miles from Norfolk. He'd been pleased to learn that Ariel's father lived in Hexham, rather than Norwich. That would keep them busy, poking up and down roads between the Wash and the Northeast. He'd also read that in 80 per cent of missing children cases a family member was involved, so the police would naturally be interested in Mr Pike. Northumberland was a tiny bit too close to Scotland for complete peace of mind, but he only had that thought in the middle of wakeful nights. During sensible daylight hours he knew there was nothing to connect him with anything found in the waters off the Western Isles. There hadn't been anything in the media about that find, the human leg bone, for weeks, either. Nothing, nothing, nothing. It was starting to feel like a well-worn and comforting mantra.

He began to feel calmer and turned his thoughts to planning their day. Perhaps he would introduce Ariel to The Story of Civilization. He owned the whole set, of course, and Ariel, demonstrating pleasure that it was shelved in her bedroom, had already examined the books and admired the picture of Will: 'He looked like a nice grandfather,' but not of his wife: 'She looks so old.' She'd been disappointed that there were no pictures of Ethel or Louis.

'We'll take pictures of our Ethel and Louis and paste them in the book then,' he'd said, somewhat surprised by his own frivolousness. She'd liked that idea. Perhaps they'd do that today. He was in the mood for something lighthearted.

He knew if he asked Ariel what she'd like to do she'd want to go out birding. He wasn't as keen. He enjoyed it only as an occasional hobby, with long fallow periods in between. It had never been one of his all-consuming passions as it looked like becoming for Ariel, if he didn't watch it. On the other hand, he didn't like to say no to her. Perhaps they could combine it with something else – wildflower identifying, maybe. That didn't hold much thrill for him either. He'd like to use the walking time to tell her more stories about the Durants' work, but knew from experience that she'd want them to be quiet, so as not to disturb the birds before she got a chance to identify them. Now that the warblers had returned she was hell bent on locating every single one possible in their area and was actually doing a pretty good job. He'd never had much luck telling them apart, but she had, it seemed to him, an unusually keen eye and an excellent memory for details.

He made himself another coffee. He must pull himself together. Ariel would be up soon and he absolutely could not involve her in his distress, or tell her his dream. Obviously she mustn't know about her predecessors. Perhaps he could just say he'd had a bad night and needed a bit of extra tenderness today. Ah, how nice it would be if he could just get into bed with her and cuddle for a while. That would soothe him. But he couldn't.

He knew that. He would ask for a hug though, on account of his sleepless night. That would be all right, he thought.

THIRTEEN

Their days settled into a familiar routine as the months of summer drifted by. Each day was much like every other day to Jessie, to the extent that they did similar things, but yet every day was also different, and seemed to offer a new and different pleasure. She'd not really had a good grasp of the days of the week before she'd met Will, and still had little interest in which day followed which. She was very aware that Will certainly knew because large parts of his routines depended on what day it was. On Sundays they changed their bed sheets and started the new week's bird list; on Mondays they counted all the loose change and Jessie carefully recorded the result in a small red cash book. On Tuesdays he backed up all his computer files and changed all the towels; Wednesdays were for housework, always done in a certain order. Thursday was shopping day and Fridays were for washing their clothes. Saturdays didn't seem to have a particular chore, but there were monthly chores too: car washing, refrigerator defrosting, window cleaning, to name a few. He didn't often get irritated about things, but Jessie could tell he didn't like it if his routines were disturbed, so she took them seriously too, and in any case, whatever they did together was enjoyable for her. She decided she'd follow his advice that if she liked, she could find out each morning what day it was from the calendar, as she entered the green, red, yellow and blue ticks, the black crosses and circles and the number of words he'd found in the polygon each day, so for a while she did just that. She could also tell by the level of the killer Sudoku, as well as their daily chore.

They usually did the polygon together over breakfast and then moved on to the Sudoku. If it was labelled 'easy' (Mondays), Will left her to it; the 'moderate', 'tricky' and 'tough' ones (Tuesdays, Wednesdays and Thursdays) they did together; and the 'deadly' ones (Friday and Saturday) he mostly did himself, though Jessie was getting better and better at seeing how it worked. She always had something to offer, occasionally before he'd seen it for himself. They never looked at the regular Sudoku. Will had told her that she was welcome to do them but he'd had no real interest since the 'killer' variety had been introduced.

'They aren't about maths; the numbers could be any symbols. I like the additional challenge of making the numbers fit the totals in the shapes. But if you want to do them I'd be more than happy to help if you need me. They are good logic puzzles and improving logical skills can only be a good thing. Though the Killer variety involves a lot of logic too, of course.'

Logic was another of Will's important things and from time to time he would set Jessie a challenge.

'You tune into a cricket match and hear the commentator saying "not a bad way to get off the mark". The score is shown on the bottom of the screen as batsman one on nineteen not out, batsman two on six not out. What just happened? Hint: batsman two is grinning.'

'He just hit a six,' scornfully. Jessie didn't need the hint; working things out based on available clues was one of her important things too. She'd spent a lifetime perfecting it.

They worked on the crossword on and off all day, and Jessie's greatest thrill came when she was able to solve a clue that Will claimed had eluded him. 'Buckled toga, velvet coat. Four letters, possibly beginning with G,' he said, as they were folding the clean clothes on a Friday afternoon. She looked at it.

'Gave!'

'Well I thought of that, but why? I can see it's there – end of toga, beginning of velvet – but it doesn't really make sense, does it?'

'It might. Can "buckled" mean gave?'

'I don't see how. Oh, wait a minute, yes, it can! Not buckle like a belt buckle, or buckle your seatbelt, it means buckle like, perhaps, a bridge that gives way, it buckles. Well done Ariel. But what directs us to look for a run-on?'

She thought he'd probably seen it by now, but she still smiled triumphantly. 'Coat. When you coat something – like a piece of fish in breadcrumbs. 'Gave' is coated by toga velvet.'

'You are so right!' and gave her a hug.

There were no special times for doing what he referred to as 'our work' – writing the next volume of the Durants' series on civilization. It came up several times each day and, as she'd known he would, Will made it interesting enough for her to enjoy their discussions about it. He'd told her not to think in terms of writing a book; that was much too big a concept. It would naturally happen, he told her, if they just kept doing what they were doing: learning about the Durants' points of view and observing their own world today. He encouraged her to write about their daily learnings and discussions in her journal and said that those writings would very likely turn into her contribution to their book. Jessie had no reason to believe this was so, but then she had no reason to believe it was not. Will had said so, and he was invariably right. She realised she was already getting used to being called Ariel by him, just has he'd said she would.

•

'What Will Durant really wanted to do was bring philosophy to the common man,' Will said. 'Until he began to do that, philosophy was thought to be something only the very educated had any truck with. To be fair to the "common man", the highly educated, and therefore "uncommon", men probably liked it that way; it made them feel special. But Will didn't think that was "fair", as you'd say. He thought everyone should be able to learn about anything they wanted to learn about, but the problem back then was that a lot of knowledge was written in such unusual – erudite is the word; we'll look that up in a minute – language that our friend, "the common man", Joe Ordinary, simply had no idea what the writers were talking about. So what do you suppose Will and Ariel did about that, my Ariel?'

'Got somebody like you to tell about it the way you tell it all to me – so I can understand it.'

'Got it in one. That's exactly what they did and that's where you come in on our project. I need to make sure you are understanding what I'm trying to say because if I talk or write over your head, then our friend Joe Ordinary isn't going to understand either.'

'He probably won't read it anyway,' Ariel obviously had memories of books that she, as Jessie, had plucked off the school

71

library shelves and that had gone right back after she'd looked at page one. 'You have to make it interesting right from the beginning.'

Will could hardly believe his ears. People spent years trying to work out how to start a book and here was Ariel, little more than a decade old, speaking a universal truth that had seemed to him known only to authors, publishers, editors and their agents. Sometimes he could hardly keep from sweeping her off her feet and hugging her so hard it would hurt. But he only smiled broadly and nodded approvingly.

'How do you think we can do that?'

He watched her thinking. He liked the way her face wrinkled up and her nostrils flared slightly, and the way the freckles on her cheeks and slightly retroussée nose almost merged as she concentrated. Unlike her namesake who had not been an attractive child, she was on her way towards growing up to be quite strikingly beautiful, he thought. For months her hair had been getting longer and longer, but two weeks ago he'd taken her to Supercuts in Burton where a trendy young stylist had given her a stunning gamine look. The cut seemed to have brightened up its somewhat mousy-red colour, and had revealed some highlights. The media photographs of 'missing Jessie' did not do her justice at all. Or perhaps she had changed since living with him all these months. That was probably more like the truth. His love and gentle attention, along with regular and healthy meals, was allowing her to unfold and blossom. He had a fleeting thought that he knew how Pygmalion had felt when he'd created his Galatea. He must tell her that story, too. She'd enjoy that. He'd tell her how the original story was created by Ovid, long before Shaw. He could even introduce her to Rameau's music for Ovid's play, as an antidote to the latter day My Fair Lady. Will felt a sudden flush of pure happiness at the realisation of just how many things there were to tell Ariel and how much they would both enjoy her pleasure in them.

'You keep talking about philosophy and civilization Will, and I don't know what you mean. P'raps Joe doesn't either.'

'Well I'm blowed! Out of the mouths... Of course you're right, that's where we need to start. Okay, our project is to work out how to get everyone to understand what it is we want them to understand about. Understand?' He was nearly delirious with joy. He'd really been talking to hear himself talk; he'd had no real expectation that Ariel would contribute at this stage. He should have known, he told himself. She was no Josephine Ordinary, far from it. 'You know what you are? You're brill!'

'I'd rather be magnificent,' she grinned at him, and helped herself to another chocolate biscuit.

FOURTEEN

'Can you swim, Ariel?' It had been stifling hot for three Indian summer days, leaving them with no energy to do anything other than lie in the shade in what passed for Will's garden: some scrubby grass, a lilac tree, a horse chestnut tree, and some nondescript bushes and brambles that he'd periodically take the shears to in attempt to forestall their taking over the whole patch. Even the now-adolescent kittens were finding it too hot to do more than swing a lazy paw occasionally at a barely moving blade of grass.

'Of course I can!' She was affronted. 'I learned when I was eight. I got my red badge straight away and then my green one the very next week. I was going to get my yellow badge pretty soon, I was nearly ready.'

'At school, was this?' She nodded. 'What did you have to do for the badges?'

'Swim a width for the red one, and do a length and a dive for the green one. You have to do three lengths for the yellow one, as well as a length in back stroke, and a dive off the low diving board. For the green one you only have to sort of fall off the edge of the pool into the water. I'm not a good diver. I can nearly do the length in backstroke though.'

'Well done you! I'm impressed. Would you like to go swimming this afternoon? We could go to Tamworth Baths – it will almost certainly be as crowded as it can get, but it might be cooling. What do you think?'

Jessie was ready and in the car before Will had time to gather his trunks and towels for them both. They stopped in the Tamworth shopping area to find something suitable for her to wear and within an hour they were in the lukewarm water, Will ploughing up and down the deep end; Jessie sliding repeatedly down the chute into the shallower end.

When they'd both had enough they sat on the balcony, watching other swimmers and divers.

'My mother used to bring me here,' Will said. 'She'd sit up here while I swam and then she'd buy me a Horlicks to warm up afterwards. They didn't heat the water much in those days.'

'P'raps we should have invited your mum to come with us today then.' Jessie would like to meet his mum.

'No, afraid not. She wouldn't be able to come.' He paused, then, 'She's dead.'

'Oh. What about your dad?'

'He's dead too, I'm afraid.'

Jessie was silent for a while, absorbing this, and trying to sort out her thoughts. Will didn't seem distressed. Should he be? 'Dad' to her was Will of course, and she couldn't imagine how she'd go on living if he died. She couldn't; she'd have to die too. She didn't think it would matter much if Milly died. Except that she wouldn't be able to show off Will to her and Jock. That would be a shame, though there'd still be David to impress. She probably wouldn't feel anything if her Norwich dad died. She'd be like Will in that. She liked that thought.

'Is everybody in your family dead then?' No wonder Will never had any visiting – or even phoning – relatives.

'Yes, they are. But it's not all bad. My parents left me enough money to live on very nicely, so I don't have to go out to work, and I don't have to worry about their wanting me to do something I don't want to do. Will Durant's mother desperately wanted him to go into the church – become a priest. I can stay at home and do the things I like to do and be with you. And you are all the family I need and want anyway.'

'You'll all the family I want, too.' Perhaps she should hug him, but something held her back, something about his damp bare chest and wet swimming trunks probably, she thought. It wouldn't feel very good. He didn't look as if he was expecting a hug anyway. She suddenly remembered.

'Can we have, I mean may we have a Horlicks?'

FIFTEEN

'May I talk to you about something Will?' She looked very serious and for a moment Will felt a flash of fear. What might be coming? But he kept his voice steady.

'Of course. Fire away.'

'Well, it's your birthday next week and I don't have any money so I can't buy you a present. And even if I did – have any money, I mean – I don't know what to buy you.'

He was touched. He couldn't remember the last time anyone had wanted to celebrate his birthday, even if it wasn't, then, on the fifth of November. 'Do you know what?' he answered, 'just having you here is birthday present enough for me. Can it be enough for you?'

'Well… no. You gave me something really special on my birthday. On both of them. I want to do the same on yours. Or at least I want to celebrate it somehow.'

'Okay, I see that. Can we have a special day in which we do things that I choose to do? Would that work for you?'

She was thoughtful for a moment. 'Yes, I think so, but I would still like to give you a surprise present.'

'I have an idea about that. Can the surprise present be doing something you choose, but you choose it because you know I'll like it, even if you don't?' He'd have liked to give her money but somehow didn't think that would fit the bill. Money for her was an issue they'd have to tackle soon, but now, he felt, was not the time.

'I think so. I'll have a think about it. I'd like to make you a cake though; can you teach me how to before next week?'

'Absolutely. Let's start today. What sort of cake do you think I'd like?'

'What kind of cake did Will Durant like? We could make that. I know – let's have a day of being the real Will and Ariel, let's do what they'd do. You'd like that.'

'I would. But it would have to be a bit different. They were married. But wait, I have an idea. Ariel roller-skated to her wedding – they got married at City Hall in New York – so let's go roller skating. Would you like to do that?' Will felt excited and hoped – prayed almost – that she would say yes.

She did. 'I think that would be terrific. I don't know if I can skate though, can you?'

'I never have, but I think we might learn together. That would be a fantastic birthday treat for me. Will that do, do you think?

It certainly would. Under Will's tutelage, she made a chocolate cake that night and a coffee cake the next day. Meanwhile Will spent long and happy hours searching and researching on the net and in his library to see if he could get a hint about what sort of cake his namesake might have liked. Although he knew that Will had not actually been named after his namesake, William James, he even searched the files for possibilities there too. In the end all he could discover was that Will's mother liked to make molasses candy so they decided that Thorntons treacle toffee would be a good substitute for that, and for the cake they settled on a Victoria sponge, simply because it was the right era.

This overt show of love was both pleasing and unsettling to Will. He didn't want to think of himself as a particularly sexual being, so was not entirely happy at the direction in which his thoughts – and his body – were tending. He did not know whether to be comforted or alarmed by reading Will Durant's account of his own experiences in that line. By the age of twelve – probably earlier – I had become an expert in masturbation. By the age of fourteen I was carrying this manual art to an extreme that alarmed my confessor. Will could gain no relief by confessing to anyone and could not tell from the earlier Will's diary account whether or not he had found any comfort in it either; whether it had helped him curtail the activity or not. All he knew was that at bedtime his body took over and his thoughts were entirely focused on a projection of his Ariel at fifteen.

SIXTEEN

His birthday had been a success he thought, as he reviewed his amazing year before drifting off to sleep on New Year's Eve. They'd had lunch in Birmingham, gone roller skating in Tamworth, and finished up at the bonfire and fireworks display at Whittington Barracks, Ariel having reminded him that this was, after all, the fifth of November and therefore Guy Fawkes' night. He'd enjoyed her telling him something for a change, and had feigned ignorance about the whole thing, although he knew she hadn't really believed him. Particularly as he'd had to help her out with some of the facts.

Yes, his birthday had been good. Christmas though, had been rather less so. He thought Ariel might be missing home but didn't like to ask her outright – he didn't want to hear her answer, he supposed, unless it was an entirely believable 'No!' She'd expressed pleasure at her presents, but sorrow that she hadn't been able to get him anything. He must do something about giving her a regular supply of money. He cursed himself for not doing anything when the subject had arisen over his birthday. Ariel repeatedly told him what a good dad he was – though she didn't actually use the word 'dad' – so why did he keep letting her down by not attending to her very real needs? Especially when they were needs that he could meet.

But that wasn't the only reason he felt Christmas hadn't gone well. Ariel had wondered, more than once it seemed, what presents David had got, and even though she'd said very quickly, 'it won't have been anything nearly as nice as mine though,' it made him uncomfortable.

And that wasn't all either. One of his presents to her had been a subscription to a birders' magazine, and it was this that seemed now to be causing some problems that he hadn't foreseen. He kicked himself for not realising that it would expose Ariel to the idea of birding in areas other than where they lived. She wanted to visit the birding hot spots, one of which, of course, was Norfolk.

'Out of the question,' he'd said, rather more curtly than he'd

78

meant to, but he was scared. 'We can't go anywhere near Norfolk, not for years, not until you've changed beyond recognition. Not unless,' he couldn't believe he was saying this, 'you want me to be arrested that is.'

Rather to his surprise she hadn't reacted this time as she had in the past; she'd matured considerably in eleven months. She hadn't become visibly upset at the thought of him languishing in jail and said, as before, 'of course we can't, I'd die if you got arrested,' or similar. She hadn't said anything, and for once in their short acquaintance Will couldn't read her; he couldn't tell if she was questioning the propriety of their relationship or if she was – in her still sometimes rather playground language, 'going off him'. This unsettled him more than anything and was undoubtedly what led to one of his 'black cross dreams' that night. And next morning he found it hard not to imply that it was all her fault, when he said, 'Black cross on the calendar this morning, I'm afraid.'

She'd put the black cross on the calendar and had been sympathetic as always – which made him feel worse. When she said, 'Shall we do something extra nice today to make up for your bad night?' he felt a total heel, so made a mammoth effort and responded, 'Yes – let's look at your birding magazine and see where we can go that isn't Norfolk but would give us a chance to see some different birds.'

They decided to go to Rutland Water, stopping at Cannock Chase on the way. As it was mid-January he didn't expect to see anything unusual, but bearing in mind that Ariel was still ticking off what to Will were basic birds, he knew it would be a good day for her, birdwise. And still not liking himself very much he said, 'And perhaps we can talk some more about the Durants on our drives.'

'Of course we can,' she seemed surprised he'd even asked. 'I never get tired of that.'

'You're a gem,' he said. 'I'm not sure I deserve you, but I'm really glad I have you.'

'Me too,' she chirped, and bustled about, getting her binoculars and bird book.

•

They'd planned to leave early, stopping for breakfast en route. They had gathered their birding equipment the night before and Will had made sure the car had a full tank of petrol and that all they'd need was already in place. Because of the cats, they would only be gone for the day – and because Will was still not quite comfortable about exposing them in hotels, even if they did have separate rooms. It was still too soon to do anything that might call attention to them.

He got up at five and was deliberately making a lot of noise in the kitchen, assuming that Ariel would hear him and get up herself. When it got to six o'clock and she hadn't appeared he went to her room, where he found her still in bed, looking decidedly off-colour.

'What's up? Are you ill?' He was concerned. One of his many middle-of-the-night anxieties was what he would do if she ever needed a doctor. Doctors were notorious for suspecting all kinds of unsavoury things when unknown children were brought to their surgeries.

She shook her head but did not speak. She certainly looked ill – more than that, she looked scared, too.

'What is it then?' He took her hand and felt her wrist. She wasn't hot. 'Did you have a bad dream?' She shook her head.

'What, then? Tell me.'

'I can't.'

'Yes you can, you can tell me anything, you know that.' Silence. 'Look, I'll sit with my back to you if you like, so you don't have to see my face, but please tell me.' More silence. He couldn't imagine what was wrong or what to do about it. You can't force a child to speak, he knew that, but he also knew he wouldn't be able to help if he didn't know what was wrong. He briefly considered a bit of emotional blackmail but he'd felt so bad about doing that the last time that he'd promised himself he would never again stoop so low. Unless he really, really had to. But what was it, what could be wrong?

'Do you want me to guess?' He couldn't stand the silence any longer.

She shook her head again. He was somewhat relieved at that;

he wouldn't even know where to start. They sat in silence again for several minutes, his mind racing. If she wouldn't tell him what was he going to do?

Then, 'I think I'm dying.'

'I'm sure you're not, but can you tell me why you think that?' He was horribly out of his depth.

'My bottom's bleeding,' and she burst into noisy tears.

SHIT! He'd been going to look on the internet to see how to tell a child about menstruation and he hadn't. Damn! He didn't have the foggiest idea what was appropriate. Oh he knew about the mechanics, he'd read plenty about how and why and all that, but what he needed was advice on how to pass on what he knew to an ignorant eleven year old. But now he had to pull himself together and reassure her first, get her to understand it was normal and later he could beat himself up all he liked.

He took her hand again. 'Listen to me Ariel, this is really important. What is happening to you is perfectly normal. It happens to all girls, starting about now and going on, once a month or so, for many years.' She stopped crying and looked at him, obviously listening and taking it in, already, he thought, looking a bit better. 'It's a signal that your body is not so much a child's body any more, but getting ready to be a woman's body so you'll be able to have babies.'

'Babies! I'm not having a baby, am I?' she began to cry again, and looked more scared than ever.

'Lord no! No, you're having what they call a period. Women – and girls – have a period every month to get rid of the stuff that your body would need inside if you were having a baby. I know it looks like blood, but really it's just the lining of your womb – where a baby would grow if you were having one. Your body realises there is no baby, so it gets rid of the lining. Like this. It's nothing to worry about, nothing at all, I promise you on my heart it isn't. In fact, it's something to celebrate, it's a sign that you are leaving childhood behind.'

She seemed reassured and content to have a bath whilst he ferreted in the boxes to find the sanitary pads. He hoped he wouldn't have to show her what to do with them but she seemed to get the idea as soon as she looked at them.

'Oh, they stick to your knickers then.' She was cheerful again; her relief was palpable.

When she was dressed and padded up they went online and looked together for information for her on the topic. They found a site that offered a book called First Moon on celebrating a girl's first period, so they ordered a copy. She liked the idea of a celebration, of course. They postponed their outing to Rutland, but he made a quick trip to the anonymous superstore near Burton, leaving Ariel in the car, to stock up on supplies for her. On the way back he told her that Ariel Durant had had a similar shock when she'd discovered herself bleeding, and that when her mother had told her she had become a woman, she had been filled with pride. His Ariel seemed to have recovered her equilibrium quickly enough and was quite ready to be equally filled with pride, but Will was heartsick to think of her lying in bed and worrying that she was dying. He hoped she wouldn't tell him he was a wonderful dad today – he felt he'd been a very inadequate dad, guardian, caretaker, prospective mate, friend, anything. He salved his conscience slightly by apologising profusely to her for not preparing her and took the opportunity to arrange a weekly income for her; money to use in any way she chose. He'd been remiss about that, too, until today.

They spent a pleasant hour or so working out her 'banking' arrangements. She wanted actual cash in hand; he wanted her to learn to manage her money on paper. In the end they compromised. He would write in her 'bank book' each week the amount she was to receive and she would convert that into cash – which he would give her and which she would keep in a battered old black cash box he'd found in his desk – whenever she wanted to.

After she'd gone to bed he allowed himself to feel more fully his horror at how he'd let her down. How selfish he'd been – wanting her for his own ends and giving no thought to her needs. He hadn't even considered what needs a young girl might have. No wonder the first two had been so stroppy and uncooperative; they'd had a better sense of themselves and what they needed from life and they'd demanded it. Ariel was too young to realise she had any rights yet. Part of his teaching must be to help her realise that she had equal rights.

Another thought struck him. Did little girls masturbate? Would he need to educate her on that score, too?

'Bloody hell,' he thought, 'she got hell from her odious stepfather for not having enough foresight – what about me! And I'm more than twenty years older than her.'

•

She would not have known that this was the one year anniversary of her disappearance if they hadn't been watching the evening news together. The next to last item was an appearance of her mother and Jock, flanked by a policeman and a policewoman. They were all sitting at a bare wooden table with glasses of water in front of them, parts of their faces hidden by what must be microphones, she thought. She looked quickly over at Will who was looking intently, worriedly, at her.

'Shall I turn it off?' He reached for the remote control.

'No-o-o, I think I want to see what they say about me, please.' She inched a little closer to him, rigid with tension.

The policeman was speaking. 'It is exactly one year ago today that young Jessie Pike disappeared on her way home from school. She was last seen by her little brother David, walking toward Summer Lane. No one has apparently seen her since.'

'That's silly,' she snorted, 'Lots of people have seen me. They just haven't told anybody.'

Will smiled and shook his head. 'It's "police speak". It means they haven't a clue what happened or where you are.'

'That's good then. I don't want them to know where I am.'

The policeman had evidently finished his speech so she watched as the scene shifted to her mother and Jock in her old house. Her eyes widened as she saw her mother sitting on a pink duvet-covered bed, surrounded by stuffed animals and dabbing at her eyes.

'I miss my little Jess,' she whimpered.

Ariel was aghast. 'Is that supposed to be my bedroom? I never had a duvet like that and I never had all those toys either. It looks more like my mother's bedroom, only the bed isn't

83

right.'

The camera moved to show Jock standing at the end of the bed, the thumb of one hand thrust into his belt and the other holding a large teddy bear by its arm.

'He's angry,' Ariel whispered. 'That's how he looks when he hits us.'

Jock leered out at her, his attempt at a smile showing his rotten front teeth that she knew smelled foul. 'Come on, Jess,' he muttered, 'Get yerself back 'ere. For yer mum.'

Will snapped the off button and moved quickly toward her as she stood up, trembling. 'Sorry, Ariel. I shouldn't have let that happen. I didn't realise it would upset you so much.' He put his arms around her and held her against him.

'It's okay.' She shuddered. 'I was thinking the other day that I missed them a little bit, but I don't think I do.'

'Not even David?'

'Well... David a bit. But to have David I'd have to have them.' She looked up at Will. 'I don't ever want to go back there Will. Please, whatever I do, please don't make me go back there.'

'Of course not. "Whither I go thou goest too," to misquote somebody.' He kissed the top of her head. 'Would you like to know how to ask "where are you going?" in Latin?'

She didn't respond.

'Quo vadis?' Silence. 'Yes, not the time for that, is it? Sorry, a silly attempt to cheer you up.' He stroked her back. 'Would you like some stuffed animals? I'm aware that you don't really have any toys here, other than things like Monopoly.'

'No thank you.' She felt – and sounded – sorrowful. Before today she might have liked a teddy or something like that, but not after seeing Jock manhandle one that was supposed to belong to her. She wondered where it had come from.

She stayed close to Will all evening, even leaving the bathroom door open whilst she had her bath, and asking him to leave her bedroom door open when he left after saying good night. She was afraid she might not be able to go to sleep. She lay perfectly still on her back and thought briefly about what it might be like to be lying, now, in that sickly pink bed, nearly suffocated by a gigantic teddy that Jock was probably going to rip the arms off.

She sighed deeply and turned onto her stomach. This was her bed. It had green checked sheets and rich brown and yellow blankets. She took a deep breath and smiled. She would never have to go back. Will had promised.

SEVENTEEN

She was wildly excited.

'Will, WILL! There's a hoopoe on our lawn, come and see.'

'No...' Disbelief. 'We don't have hoopoes here, it can't be, Ariel, it must be an ordinary jay.'

She knew he was wrong for once. 'It isn't, it's a hoopoe. And we can get them here. Well, in places in England anyway, I read about it in Birding Magazine. Come and see... oh, it's gone. Well maybe it will come back. Birding says they like vicarage lawns, I wonder why. Our lawn isn't like a vicarage lawn, I'd say.'

'No indeed. It's hardly like a lawn at all. But if it is a hoopoe, maybe it's here because you are – it's come because it knows you'll appreciate it. Or maybe it's just wishful thinking on your part?'

'You don't believe me. I can tell by your smile – and the way you are talking. Look, it says they come here at this time of year from Scandinavia – where's that?' She was immediately back in familiar and comfortable territory, student to his teacher. She listened to Will's explanation and together they looked at the map, but she still wasn't willing to believe that it was impossible that the bird in question would come this far south. She was sure she'd seen one, even if Will didn't believe it.

She wanted to stay outside, waiting and watching, but Will wanted them to work on their 'project'. For the first time ever she didn't want to talk about Will and Ariel Durant – she wanted to talk about hoopoes.

'I've always found it interesting,' he said, 'that although the Durants desperately wanted to improve people's understanding of other viewpoints, different from theirs, and wanted others to be more understanding of what they called human frailties and waywardness – I'll explain that in a minute – when they wrote their Story of Civilization they could be a bit harsh. They wrote a lot about what they called "the dominance of strong over the weak" and "the clever over the simple". Do you see any conflict there, Ariel?'

'No.' She knew that was the right answer, the answer Will wanted, so she gave it, hoping they could go back to watching for the hoopoe. But it wasn't good enough

'Perhaps we need to explore what those words mean first,' he said, and launched into an explanation of frailties, waywardness and finally dominance. Ariel thought sulkily she could offer a very good example of dominance right now, if he asked. But he didn't. Instead he said: 'What the Durants were trying to do was create what they called "integral history", including not just the usual wars, politics and biographies of greatness, but also culture, art, philosophy, religion and the rise of mass communication. Will felt that writing about each aspect separately only ended up shredding history. He was determined to weave all the strands together to make what he called the "complex web of civilization". Rather like what I've been trying to do with you – teach you things from all these areas so you are a well-rounded scholar, not just an expert. Am I succeeding, do you think?'

She had no idea, but she didn't see why being well rounded couldn't include learning more about birds and birding. She pressed her lips together in a straight line and thought briefly, with surprise, that she couldn't remember the last time she'd done that, put on her 'stubborn face'.

'I like learning, Will. Today I especially like learning about birds.' She paused, sensing his displeasure at her changing the subject. So, 'Did Will and Ariel know about birds?' She felt Will might be more inclined to pay attention to the possibility of a hoopoe on their lawn if the Durants had had any interest in birds.

'I don't remember reading anything about that, but they might have, I suppose. They made a point of being interested in everything, after all. Shall we do some research on the web this afternoon? There was a very famous American who identified and painted birds – the Durants would certainly have known of him, though he lived a good fifty years before they were born. We'll look him up; his name was John James Audubon. Look, here's a book of his watercolours of the birds of America.'

Jessie couldn't put it into words but she felt the breach was healed. They were 'back together' again, is how she put it to herself. And she was relieved. She'd always seemed to be falling out with her mother or Jock or David, or all three, and she felt very uncomfortable at the possibility that she and Will might have such a falling-out. Especially over something as important as their 'project' – or her interest in birds.

•

'Have a look at this, Ariel,' Will was at the computer where he'd found a photofit of what the missing Jessie might look like, one year and thirty-plus days on since she was last seen in Sheringham. 'It doesn't look anything like you.'

Ariel had to agree. This was a little girl, whereas she was actually a quite mature-looking young teen now.

'I would never have had my hair like that,' she was outraged at the childish plaits. 'It's nerdy. And I wouldn't have worn a dorky jumper like that, either.' She wasn't really unhappy that they'd got it so wrong, but all the same there was something unsettling about seeing this picture of how people in Sheringham were thinking of her when she knew she was now so different. Even if she wanted to – and she certainly didn't – she could never go back now.

'It says I'm twelve today. I suppose I am really. Are we going to celebrate my real birthday?'

'I hadn't planned to – you're Ariel Dee now and your "real" birthday is on the tenth of May.' He looked closely at her. 'Do you mind not having a birthday celebration today?'

She did mind, but could see Will had not even thought about it, so she shook her head. 'Not really. Well, a little bit, I suppose. I still think of me as having my birthday on the fifth of March.'

'Of course you do! I'm sorry, Ariel, that was really thoughtless of me. Sometimes I'm not nearly as in tune as I ought to be. Let's do something special, even though we aren't strictly speaking celebrating your birthday – what would you like to do?'

'Could we go birding? She had no hesitation. 'Birding says the chiffchaffs should be here. I'd like to see one for my Life

List.'

'Of course we could – where shall we go? I know, let's go and look at the vicarage and see if your hoopoe is on the vicar's lawn.' He grinned at her.

She glared back. 'Oh I know you don't believe me. One day I'll surprise you though. You'll see.'

'You surprise me daily, Ariel. I had never imagined life with you could be so interesting and rewarding. And you know what, nothing would make me happier than to find a hoopoe on our lawn. Especially today.'

While it was pleasant to hear him say that, she didn't really believe it; which was another unsettling thought. Had she known the word, she might have thought he was being condescending. As it was, she just thought he was being 'like a grown up'.

'Crikey,' she mused, 'does turning twelve mean you see things more? If that's true, then I think I'll be happy to be eleven for a lot longer.'

They didn't see a hoopoe – or a chiffchaff – but they did have a good time, ending up at Goli's in Lichfield for a pizza supper. All the same, Jessie went to bed feeling a bit let down and couldn't immediately fall asleep. There seemed to be an increasing number of occasions lately when she and Will weren't quite 'in tune' as he would put it. Was it her fault? Was it only over the birding, or was he finding her difficult in other ways? Now that she thought about it, he didn't seem as keen to hug her as he used to be. Nor did he hug her as closely. She sighed and turned onto her other side. She'd struggled to write about these thoughts in her journal and then been anxious that Will's feelings might be hurt if he read it. She'd pushed it under her mattress to keep it out of sight and, hopefully, out of Will's mind. If David were in the next bedroom she would have gone in to talk to him about it. Not that he'd give her any answers, he never had. But it would have been nice to talk to someone other than Will for a change. Especially about Will.

'And about birding,' she muttered rebelliously, and went to sleep.

•

She hadn't drawn her curtains last night, so the early morning spring light streaming in woke her earlier than usual. Will wouldn't be up for ages, maybe she'd go out by herself and see if there were any spring birds to watch. Come to think of it, she'd learned from the magazine that dawn was a really good time to see birds you might not see later in the day.

She dressed quickly and quietly let herself out of the back door with her binoculars and bird book. The magazine was right. She immediately saw two male blackbirds digging furiously for worms just under the bushes. There were ten or more chaffinches hopping about; loads of tits of all kinds, two nuthatches – she'd only ever seen one before – and a pair of collared doves on the lawn. Had it been a dove she'd seen yesterday, pretending to be a hoopoe? No, she knew she wouldn't have made such a simple mistake. It could have been an ordinary jay; she'd admit that. And it could have been wishful thinking as Will had suggested. She was honest enough to admit that, too.

She moved slowly down the drive, stopping frequently to peer through her binoculars into the bushes lining the driveway. She didn't see anything new, but there was a lot to watch and she was thrilled to see and hear a wren making far more noise than she'd have thought possible from that tiny frame. It – a 'he' probably, she thought, singing to attract a mate – moved to another bush, so she followed slowly, anxious not to alarm it, but keen to see and hear more. She didn't realise she was at the end of their drive until the post van pulled up for the postman to put their mail into the wooden box. She thought briefly about hiding, but it would have seemed silly, she thought. Besides, he'd obviously already seen her.

'Morning,' he said, through his rolled-down window. 'You live around here?'

She nodded.

'Well it must be right here then – there's no other houses on this road for two miles or more.' He seemed friendly enough, but Ariel felt sure Will wouldn't like her talking to him. He'd been quite firm about her not talking to the girl who cut her hair in Supercuts. Not that she'd found that difficult – she'd been tongue-tied and the girl had been busily singing along to the strange music piped into the salon.

'Do you want to take the post – it's all addressed to Mr Dee?'

She nodded again. Then couldn't resist it. 'He's my dad.'

'Is he? I didn't know he had kids. You just visiting then?'

'No,' proudly, 'I live here. I live here with my dad.'

'Well I never. And I've never seen you. Well I'll be seeing you again then. Here you go, here's the post. Not much of it and what there is, is junk. Nobody seems to write to your dad. Or to you for that matter, though one of you did get that big pink envelope not so long ago – what's your name, anyway?'

'Je-Ariel. Ariel Dee. But I haven't lived here always. I used to live in… in… somewhere else.' She suddenly sensed the danger but the postman seemed oblivious to her hesitation. He handed the rubber-banded-together packet of post to her, rolled up his window, tooted his horn and drove away.

•

Will had been startled by the difference in the projected, photofit image of what Ariel might look like now and how she actually looked. As she'd been quick to point out, 'Jessie' was a child, whereas Ariel was almost, if not quite, a young woman. She'd never been chubby, but her babyish cheeks had slimmed to a soft beauty and she'd grown several inches; or so it seemed to him. He'd recently noticed small swellings under her t-shirt and saw, when they went swimming, hair under her arms. Presumably she was growing pubic hair too. He hadn't commented – should he? Was it lazy to leave it to her to bring up the subject? Or was that the right thing to do? He hoped so, but the memory of her horror at starting her first period in ignorance – because of him – had not quite left him.

Perhaps she was getting information from the book they'd sent for. She'd certainly been keen to read it and 'over the moon,' she'd declared, to get post for herself, addressed, like her birding magazine, to A.Dee. He hoped she wouldn't now get on all sorts of junk mail lists, but it couldn't be helped. He'd had to get her the book.

Would it be inappropriate to ask her if he could read it? Then perhaps they could discuss these things? He felt sure she would agree immediately, but he wasn't so sure that he would be able to detect reluctance if there were some. Looking back over the last – what – two, three months, he realised there had been a subtle shift in her attitude towards him. Not antagonism, never that, but an imperceptible – at the time – withdrawal that left him now feeling acutely uncomfortable. There was also a small but growing tendency on her part to have different opinions from his. That was probably a good thing, he told himself firmly, but he'd enjoyed her 'rubber-stamping' his views all the time. Part of him still felt that was how it ought to be anyway. That's how Ariel Durant had been with her Will.

He wished he hadn't laughed at her over the damn hoopoe. Even more, he wished she weren't quite so keen on pursuing her bird watching career to the extent of spending longer periods away from him, in the garden. And, probably because he had laughed at her hoopoe, she no longer told him what she had seen there. She would simply come in, put her binoculars and bird book away, and join him in whatever he was doing.

The other day he'd gone into the kitchen and she'd been there on the telephone. He'd been shocked – who was she talking to? – but waited until she said goodbye and hung up.

'Who were you talking to?' He tried not to sound agitated.

'The BTO.' She seemed pleased, triumphant almost. 'I wanted to ask them if it was possible for a hoopoe to be here. They said it was.'

Here! What had she told them? He took a deep breath. 'Where did you say "here" was?'

'I said in the Midlands. I knew you wouldn't want me to say Whittington so when he asked if it was East or West Midlands, I said we were a bit near Burton and a bit near Birmingham. He said in any case it was possible, but not likely. Was it all right that I used the phone?'

'I'd rather you asked, Ariel. I'm sure I'll always say yes, but you might not be as aware as I am of what these things might lead to. But no harm done in this instance.' He hoped.

She was being secretive, he thought. She's not letting me in to all corners of her life, as she should. She hadn't shown him her journal for a couple of weeks. Come to think of it, he hadn't noticed it around lately, either. Ariel Durant always gave her writings to Will for his corrections and approval. And in turn, she reviewed his contributions. Each of them sanctioned the whole; they kept nothing from each other. They had written proudly about this sharing. How had his Ariel begun to drift from him? Was it something he had done or not done, or was it simply in her nature and therefore nothing could be done about it? He couldn't believe that. Ariel Durant had described herself as very much like her own mother, 'who was stranger than fiction', and yet allowed and encouraged her husband to 'supply what was left out of her hereditary makeup' for over sixty-three years. She'd felt no need to hide from him. Nor, apparently, he from her.

'And you are being secretive yourself, Will Dee,' he suddenly said to himself. You aren't telling her that you are having very un-fatherly feelings about her new body and that hugging her as of old is giving you an erection that is hard to hide. You've started withdrawing – and wearing baggy jogging bottoms to cover your embarrassment. And you know she notices the change. That's probably why she's pulling back a little; she perceives it as something you want.

Oh Christ! Never mind a book for her, he needed a book on how to turn a ten-year-old child into a fourteen-year-old bride. He was confident no such book existed. But maybe together, later, they would write one. That was an encouraging thought.

•

She told herself she didn't know why she hadn't told Will about meeting the postman, but there was never a moment's doubt that she must not tell him. She knew he would not be pleased at all, and pleasing Will was still vitally important to her.

As the mornings got lighter and lighter, earlier and earlier, she found it was quite easy to wake early and be at the end of the driveway when the postman came. She liked their brief chats and always hoped there would be a way to work in a mention of 'her dad'. She liked the sound of it. The postman didn't always come – there wasn't always any post for Will – but he'd usually

93

toot his horn and wave as he drove by. And when he did come, he always handed her what little there was, and she always waited until he'd gone, and then dropped it into the locked box. She didn't want Will to know she'd been anywhere near the end of the drive, but thought if he did find out she'd simply say she was following what she thought was a hoopoe. Being plausible came easily. She'd leave the postman out of it.

In any case, it was part of Will's unvaried late-morning routine to walk up the driveway to collect his post. He would not have liked that routine disrupted any more than he liked his other invariable habits altered. He'd said as much. 'It gives me a certain amount of comfort to put the clean towels at the bottom of the stack, Ariel, and use them in order. It might be seen as a little obsessive, but it does no harm.' He'd winked at her. 'So humour me.' She was more than happy to do so. Humouring Will was top of her list of important things. She just wished it didn't un-humour him that she was so passionately interested in birds. Or should that be dis-humour? She'd ask him, he loved being asked things like that.

Actually, he loved being asked anything – with the possible exception of details about his dead cousin Sally or any of the rest of his family. But apart from wondering very briefly why Sally's clothes were in a box marked A-II and not S-something, Ariel didn't really care about the owner of the clothes. In any case, she'd outgrown most of them already, and accumulated a lot of other things of her own choosing. Will was quick to say he had no knowledge about girls' clothes so would she please choose whatever she wanted and he would pay for it – and please remember to put the new things under the clothes already in the drawers, and wear them in their proper order. He'd been fine about her ordering some bras on line– and having to send them back because they weren't the right size. He'd even been okay about having to do it three times before she got what she felt was right. It hadn't occurred to Ariel that it might have been easier if she'd gone into a shop and tried them on before buying. If it had occurred to Will he hadn't said anything about it.

Most of all he liked being asked about the Durants. So on the mornings she'd met and chatted with Harry the postie – they were on first name terms now – she usually salved her conscience by bringing up the topic of their heroes.

'Was that the first time they met then, when he was her teacher?' Ariel couldn't imagine fancying any of the old codgers she'd had at her school, but if Will Durant was anything like Will Dee, then that might be different. Very different. 'Did she think he was handsome?'

'Alas, no. She has written that she thought he looked a bit ridiculous. He was quite short, you know, about five foot five, that's only about an inch taller than you. He had nice black hair, she said, but a pink and blotchy face.'

'Yuck! Not a bit like you then.' Ariel thought Will was quite likely the most handsome man she'd ever seen, with his dark brown hair, brown eyes, and what she thought of as his nice round face. Not fat, she emphasised to herself, just nice and round.

'No, but evidently she could see beneath looks and fell in love with something more important I suppose. At any rate, she fell for him and actually tried to kiss him in the playground. It turned out later that he had similar feelings for her, but in the first place thought this was just a typical teenage crush phase Ariel was going through and in the second place very mindful of their age difference and what people might think.'

'Did she kiss him on the lips?' Ariel was fascinated.

'I think she was trying to, but he pushed her away.'

'When I'm fourteen will I be allowed to kiss you? On the lips?'

'Absolutely. If you still want to. We'll have to wait and see if you still want to.'

She was very conscious of some strange feelings in the pit of her belly and wondered if her period had come again. It wasn't a bad feeling, but it was strange.

•

Bloody hell! Will thought. How did Will Durant stand it? He'd only been twenty-seven and her coming full on at him, 'close at hand, crazy with life and energy, and physically in full bloom' as she had described herself. He's stronger stuff than I am.

Fourteen. How many months, weeks, days, till she was

fourteen? Over two years, anyway. Sneering slightly at himself, he took his small date book out of his pocket and counted. Dare he put the number of days on the calendar in the kitchen, where he kept all other such trivial yet also important information? She'd know, she'd know that's what it was. And would it be when she was really fourteen on the fifth of March or did he have to wait until the tenth of May? Hoist by my own petard there, he told himself wryly.

They were watching a one-day international cricket match, coming to them from Sri Lanka. Will had attempted to tell Ariel about the Durants' visit to Sri Lanka and their hopes that education there would someday replace fear as the basis for morality and social order, but Ariel was glued to the screen, anxious for her hero, the shaggy-haired bowler, to hit the winning runs before he was summarily dismissed.

'A walking wicket, that's what he is,' she said, echoing the commentators as she so often did. But because she was so riveted, he was free to look at her all he liked, comparing her – as Will had compared his Ariel – with Shelley's wild west wind, 'tameless and swift and proud'. Her breasts were more than mere swellings now. They were very definite small mounds. They made him think of Ariel Durant's account of how Will had first kissed her breasts – before they were married – and how he always remembered the exact date and re-enacted the event every year on that date. Oh lucky Will! Meantime, should he ask his Ariel if she needed – or wanted – more bras? He knew he didn't need to; she'd been completely matter-of-fact about getting her first supply, even laughing at herself for getting ones that were first too big and then too small before she'd finally got what they called her Goldilocks set: just right. He'd had a struggle to match her nonchalant attitude when he'd been dying to get involved. Will Durant hadn't had that problem, but then he'd had to deal with a family who vehemently opposed his relationship with the Jewish Chaya, as she'd originally been named. Will had anglicised it to Ida, then nicknamed her Puck, and finally rechristened her Ariel. He wondered if Will Durant had realised that he'd named her after two male fairies. He must have. Will smiled sardonically to himself; he was quite sure Ariel's parents had not knowingly named the baby Jessie after Shylock's daughter though. He considered telling Ariel about it; she might like the (extremely tenuous) Jewish connection and she'd definitely like the story of the pound of flesh and how the clever Portia, disguised as lawyer Balthazar, had resolved it. But no; Will couldn't bring himself to remind her of her original name. He must keep moving her forward to her new destiny.

'I'd love to go to Sri Lanka,' Ariel interrupted his thoughts. 'We could see the elephant orphanage and all sorts of birds we'd never see in England.'

'Ah that would be nice... But we can't go abroad unless we can find a way to get you a passport, that's the problem. It's all very well you and me saying you are Ariel Dee, but the powers-that-be would want to see some proof, things like a birth certificate.'

'And we couldn't even get me a passport as Jessie Pike either – they'd want to know where I've been all this time.' Ariel went straight to the heart of the matter as usual. 'Never mind, maybe we'll think of something one day. Maybe you'll think of something, I mean.'

And having re-affirmed her faith in his power to conquer all, she turned her attention back to the cricket.

EIGHTEEN

'It's my birthday today, Harry.' She was at the post box bright and early on the tenth of May, hoping there would be post for Will so that Harry would come.

'All right! Happy birthday. How old are you?'

'Twelve. I'll be thirteen next year.'

'Well blow me down, I'd have thought you were older than that now. You look nearer to fourteen, to me.' He looked her over, appraisingly. 'No post for you, though – how come your mates haven't sent you any cards?'

'Oh.' She was taken aback. This was unexpected – and dangerous. 'Maybe they don't know it's my birthday. I expect that's it. Well, I'd better be going in.'

'You lot don't get much in the way of interesting post, do you. I suppose the bird mag is for you. I know we ain't supposed to look, but we can't help noticing what people get, can we? We see it all. We know who gets things in plain brown wrappers, even if we don't know exactly what's inside. We can make a pretty good guess though. We usually read the postcards too; mind you, your dad don't get any postcards – or letters. Which doesn't upset me; frankly I'd rather not stop on this nasty corner anyway. Here, don't forget the post – junk again, I'm afraid.' He thrust the wad into her hand as she set off back down the drive.

Halfway to the house she realised she was still holding it. Should she take it back to the box? What if Harry was still there; she hadn't heard his van leave. She looked at it. Was there anything important? Important enough for Will to have today? She could hide it and put it in the box tomorrow, then she wouldn't have to go back to the box, or let Will know she'd seen the postman.

She stuffed the three envelopes and a supermarket flyer under a bush and ran back to the house. They were going to Edgbaston for the day, to see a county cricket match. She'd have liked to see an international team, but Will was concerned that an important match like that would be televised, and he hadn't wanted to risk their being seen on television. Not that anyone would recognise her now, she was sure, but cricket was cricket and she knew she would enjoy the day out no matter what.

Will was up when she went into the kitchen.

'Happy birthday, Ariel,' he sang out. 'How does it feel to be twelve now?'

Not actually feeling any different – and bearing in mind that as far as she was concerned she'd actually turned twelve over two months ago – she just smiled and sat at her place to eat. There was a large white envelope propped against her cup. A card! She must be sure to tell Harry next time she saw him that her dad had made sure she got a card.

She opened it. Not surprisingly it was a picture – black and white and photocopied – of Ariel Durant at about twelve or thirteen. Will had obviously made the card himself using a picture he'd found online, she supposed. Inside he had written 'I love you, dear, for what you are and for what you are going to be – my wild, sweet, radiantly healthy, divinely terrible, Walt Whitman girl. Will.'

She looked at him. 'What's a Walt Whitman girl?'

'He's the next chapter in our learning: he's an American poet that the Durants greatly admired. Largely because Whitman also had a great interest in bringing poetry to what he called "the common man". Remember, the Durants' passion was to make things understandable to "Joe Ordinary". Walt Whitman was also interested in something called "free love" – as were the Durants of course. I rather think Will was teaching about Whitman to Ariel's class. No, she actually knew about him before she met Will. Her mother taught her about Whitman, not to mention other famous authors – we'll get to them all eventually – like Tolstoy. Unlike you, though through no fault of yours, Ariel did not come to her Will naïve and ignorant. Anyway, those are his words, Will's, but I don't think he'd mind in the least that I borrowed them. They are so apt for you. Don't you think?'

'Thank you Will. I love you, too.' She got up to hug him and was pleased that he stood up too, and held her very close. She couldn't be sure, but she thought he kissed her hair. He certainly nuzzled her neck.

•

'Did you know there's a girl living with that Dee man out at the Moor?' Harry was sorting the post in the back room of the village post office. Mrs Simmons, the postmistress, had just bought him a cup of tea and a biscuit. A custard cream today, his favourite. Hers too, she'd put several on her own saucer.

'No! What sort of a girl? A girl-friend?'

'No, she says she's his daughter. I didn't know he was married – well maybe he isn't, these days folk have kids without benefit of clergy as we say in the trade. She told me it was her birthday the other day – she was twelve, she said, though she looks quite a bit older to me.'

'Well I never. You don't see him much in the village, do you? I can't remember the last time he came in here. Oh yes I can, it was to ask about the Leedses' kittens. He took two, Mrs Leeds told me, but she never said anything about a daughter. I'll have to ask her. D'ya want another cup, Harry? I think I can squeeze one more out of this pot.'

'No, ta. Too much means I've gotta stop somewhere to relieve the old bladder. I used to count on doing it by the Dee's drive, but these days the girl is always there when I get there.'

'You'd better not be unzipping yourself in front of no twelve-year-olds, Harry West. You can get put away for a tidy while for doing that.' She said it almost unthinkingly, part of her daily banter with the sixty-year-old postman, but the thought stayed with her for most of the day. Not about Harry, no way, that wasn't his scene at all – his passion was his rose garden. But what about the girl and her father? It all sounded very fishy to her, though she couldn't say why it should. Where had she come from and how come nobody ever saw her? Mrs Simmons decided to make sure she was in the post office the next time Mrs Leeds came in. She'd soon get to the bottom of this.

•

Things were better between him and Ariel. Whatever had briefly blighted their togetherness seemed to have disappeared, much to

Will's relief. Now if only his nightmares would go away, permanently. While Ariel was in the bath one evening he looked back through the calendar to confirm his suspicion that the black crosses were coming more frequently lately. They were. Why? What could be causing that? Last night's had been a particularly bad one and so vivid that it had taken him some thirty minutes to fully grasp that it was just a dream. It had been so real. He had smelled the oily ferry and tasted the salty spray as he stood on the deck, waiting for the right moment to dispose of his bundle. If only the girls weren't so alive in the dream. In reality it had been so peaceful and quiet, but in his dreams they screamed and screamed and screamed. And more often than not, when he woke up, he found it was he who was screaming. Thank God it never woke Ariel, though lord knows he could have done with some comforting and a dose of her normality.

Perhaps he was suffering from posttraumatic stress disorder. That seemed to be the disorder of the times, according to newspapers. Certainly what he had done was extremely traumatic and he'd never talked about it to anyone. Of course he hadn't! How could he? But perhaps he could find help on the internet. 'The web is your friend...' he reminded himself, having said it many times to Ariel when she was puzzling over something.

He made himself some strong coffee and decided to stay up all night. The benefits would be twofold: no chance of a bad dream, and he might very well find something helpful online.

What should he type in as a keyword? Not 'murder'. He couldn't face that. Okay, how about 'death'? Too vague. Too many millions of hits. Posttraumatic stress disorder – PTSD seemed to be its recognisable abbreviation – gave him almost as many, but it was easy enough to navigate through until he found some useful resources. Books, there were plenty of books that could help. But he didn't fancy either ordering them online or going into a bookshop to buy them. Silly, really, people bought books on all manner of subjects without the shop staff batting an eye. But he knew he couldn't face it.

Following a 'suggested treatments' thread, he came across EMDR, a system of eye movements devised in America that was said to have miraculous results in helping PTSD sufferers store their traumas more appropriately in their brains, thus taking the intensity out of the experience. He read for a couple of hours about that. The only trouble was, you had to go to a trained practitioner, and naturally you had to tell them what was causing your trouble.

But wait. The woman who had discovered – or invented – the technique, had done it on herself. So why couldn't he? It was certainly worth a try. He read more about Francine Shapiro, how she had switched her eyes from side to side repeatedly whilst out walking and felt her angst lift. Worth a try, he thought. So now more coffee and tomorrow, as soon as it's daylight, out I go.

•

'I'm not much taken with Walt Whitman, Will,' Ariel said. 'I must be honest.'

'What are you reading?'

'Something called Perfections. "Only themselves understand themselves and the like of themselves, As Souls only understand Souls." I can't make out what he's saying.'

'It does seem a very roundabout way to say "like belongs with like", or that people with similar likes and dislikes enjoy each other more than people with different opinions. You know—birds of a feather flock together? But that's a bit of a difficult concept for you, when he puts it so strangely. Try reading the one called On the Beach at Night. It's still sometimes very strange language, but it's about a child standing on the beach with her father – you can relate to that, I fancy.'

She read it carefully.

'Like that better?' he asked when she looked up.

'A bit. It's still a very strange way to tell a story, but it's not as bad as some of them.'

'Yes, I know what you mean, he's hard to read. And if the truth were told, he's trying to get messages across in his poetry without actually saying them, which makes him even harder to understand.'

'Why doesn't he just come right out and say things then?' For all her deceit about talking to the postman, and her history of being necessarily careful with the truth when the occasion arose, her basic instinct was to be honest. Especially with Will, who so rarely told her off. With Jock and her mother it had been a different story; then lying had been a matter of self-preservation. But that had been Jessie. Now she was Ariel, and different. Better different.

'Ah, because what he was saying would not have been received very well. The idea of "free love" was not an easy concept for people to grasp, even if they were indulging in it behind closed doors. But even more hidden in his words, so some people believe, is an endorsement – a blessing on – homosexuality. Do you know what that is?'

She shook her head.

'Being gay. Does that mean anything to you?'

'Oh yes. Lots of people in my school said the Angel twins were gay because they went about together all the time. I think it's because they were twins and were used to being together all the time.'

'Yes. Well, when Walt was a young man, being gay was not only unacceptable but it was also against the law. So he was being very brave in even hinting at it. But we needn't concern ourselves with that aspect. It's the body electric, universal brotherhood and the free love bit we are interested in, because that's what the Durants were interested in.'

'They weren't gay, were they? They were married.' Ariel focused on the only bit of Will's response that she could understand at all.

'Some people think Ariel Durant might have been, but I don't think so. I think she was just shy about showing her love as passionately as Will did.'

'She wasn't shy about kissing him on the lips though.'

'No, she wasn't.'

'What is free love, Will?'

'Ah. Let's have lunch first. Free love is a big topic for us. We're going to need most of the afternoon to get through it well. Meanwhile, it's enough to remember that it was the idea of a group of people who rejected the concept of marriage. They thought that love alone could bind two people together. They didn't need the church to sanction it.'

'Like us then. We love each other but we don't go to church about it.'

'Yes. Rather like us.'

NINETEEN

Will had dosed off in front of his computer after his discovery of EMDR, and had overslept the following morning, so, not wanting to have to explain to Ariel what he was doing, it wasn't until two days later that he took himself outside to walk briskly up and down the drive, holding the disturbing dream image in his mind and shifting his eyes from left to right and back again.

He didn't know what to expect so, sensibly, told himself to expect nothing. All the same, he was surprised to see a stash of wet and crumpled paper under a scruffy rosemary bush. He reached in to get it, thinking he'd put it in the bin when he got back to the house. To his amazement, it was his post; rather damp for being there, but his post nonetheless: a 'To the Occupier' envelope, a 'special offer' from The Economist, what looked like an appeal from the Royal National Institute for the Blind and the weekly specials flyer – from a week or so ago – from Tesco. Why was it there? It obviously had been placed there, anchored by a stone – it hadn't just been blown there by the wind. But by whom?

He crumpled up the paper and crammed it, with the envelopes, into his windbreaker pocket and continued his walk, trying to concentrate on his left-right-left eye movements. He must be seeing things – for a split second he thought he saw Ariel in the driveway, but he was mistaken. She wasn't there. When he got to the end of the drive, however, he was just in time to see the post van pull up.

'Good morning.'

'Morning, squire. Want your post?'

'Yes, thanks. Not much of interest probably.'

'No, I suppose not, though I never look. I just see the name and put it in the box – or more likely give it to your daughter. She's usually up here looking for birds when I come by.'

'My daughter? You usually give the post to my daughter?' He couldn't believe his ears. 'But, I come up here and get it from the box.' He became aware that the old postman was looking at him rather oddly, so shook his head. 'Well, on the days she doesn't bring it to the house of course.' It was suddenly clear. Ariel had been getting the post but had not brought it to him. Rather, she'd left it in the box for obvious reasons: she hadn't wanted him to know she was talking to the postman.

'Well, thanks. Bye.' He turned on his heel and strode back to the house. That could have been Ariel in the driveway then. And, come to think of it, that's how come his post from the some time ago had ended up under a bush. Though why, he couldn't imagine. And it didn't really matter. What mattered was finding out just what Ariel had told the blasted postman. Didn't she know it was dangerous to talk to strangers?

The irony of that hit him and he almost laughed.

'Right. Must stay calm. No sense attacking her.' He must proceed very carefully here, but at the same time, he must put a stop to her dalliance with the blasted postman. That had been Ariel he'd thought he'd seen earlier. His sudden appearance on the driveway at that hour of the day must have shocked her horribly.

'Not nearly as horribly as she's shocked me though,' he muttered grimly to himself as he went back into the house.

•

Mrs Simmons didn't have to wait long for Mrs Leeds to come into the post office. As she expected, the primary school teacher came in on Tuesday to post her Ebay packages. The portly Mrs Simmons went straight to the point, foregoing her usual nosiness about what had been sold and how much money Mrs Leeds was making by selling off her unwanted knick-knacks. 'You know that Mr Dee what lives out at the Moor, him as got the two kittens off you?'

'Well, I know who you mean. I wouldn't say I know him. What about him?'

'Well then, Harry West reckons he's got a girl living with him – a teenager. Says it's his daughter. I suppose that's why he wanted the kittens.'

'I suppose so, though he didn't say anything at the time. I did wonder, but didn't like to ask.'

'No, you don't, do you. But it seems odd, don't it, that nobody ever sees her.'

'I wonder where she goes to school.' Mrs Leeds had a genuine interest in that. She was deputy head of the infants' school and her husband was a department head in the secondary school. 'I'll ask Bill if she goes to school here.'

Mrs Simmons was pleased. She hadn't thought of that. It might be illegal for the girl not to be going to school. Mrs Simmons didn't wish anybody any harm, but she liked a bit of scandal as much as the next person.

'If she doesn't go to our school, where else could she go?'

'Oh, anywhere. She could go to boarding school – that'd be why we never see her. Or she might be home-schooled. But I will ask Bill. You've got me curious now.'

Mrs Simmons pressed on. 'Too right. These days you never know, do you? It seems odd to me that a nice-looking young man like him lives out there all alone – and then suddenly produces a full-grown daughter. Makes you think.'

'What does it make you think, Mrs S? Are you suggesting he's up to no good?'

'You never know,' Mrs Simmons said darkly. 'You never ever know.'

•

'I thought you said Jessie was ten when she went missing, Milly?' Agnes was helping her neighbour clear out the last of Jessie's belongings so David could finally call her old room his own. In the little chipboard desk she'd found Jessie's birth certificate, and being uncontrollably nosy, had looked at it. What she was really curious about was to see if Milly had actually been married to Howard when she got pregnant, but she hadn't expected to find out that Jessie had actually been born a full year before Milly had said she was.

'According to this, she would have been eleven then. So she'd be twelve, no, thirteen now. She's had two birthdays.'

'I suppose so. Doesn't matter though, does it?' Milly was her usual distracted, distant, self. Agnes had wondered to Les if Milly might be 'on something'.

'Don't be daft,' he'd responded. 'She's always been a bit light between the ears, that one.'

'Well it might. For instance the made-up pictures the police artist did to show what she might look like now won't be very realistic. She'll be a teenager now – with boobs, I shouldn't wonder, if she takes after you. You ought to phone that police lady what's been working on the case and tell her.'

'Oh I don't think it's worth it. They think she's dead now anyway. They've as good as told me to think of her that way and get on with my life, even though they keep saying they're still hoping and looking and I mustn't give up hope. Jock's sure she's dead.'

'And how would Jock know? Does he have a direct line to the other side then? Or maybe he knows more about it all than he wants you to think.' Agnes rarely missed an opportunity to have a dig at Jock. She still hadn't forgiven him for his brutal treatment of the ultra-sensitive David. And when they'd been staying in her house whilst the police fine-tooth-combed Jock and Agnes's place, she'd told him as much, and threatened to tell the police if he didn't stop it. To her amazement, he'd crumpled under her attack, as bullies often do, and promised on his life he'd never touch the kid again if Agnes would only not tell on him. Agnes had been stunned, and very pleased at her ability to wield a little power. It went a long way towards easing the ache inside that came from knowing how much her Les still fancied the bubble-headed Milly.

'Jock thinks he knows everything,' Milly said.

TWENTY

Ariel had raced back to the house, terrified that Will might have seen her. She was shaking as she put her binoculars and bird book away, but tried to reassure herself. 'He probably didn't see me. And even if he did, I wasn't doing anything wrong.' But she knew she was, so being defiant wasn't an option. She knew that talking to the postman and revealing what little she had revealed would very definitely be wrong in Will's eyes.

What would he say? What would he do? Would he hit her? For a hot and frantic moment she thought about running away, but instantly dismissed the idea as stupid. There were only two directions she could go and Will would of course come looking for her in his car. If he didn't come across her going one way he'd turn around and find her going the other way. And anyway, where could she run to? It wasn't like last time when she'd a destination in mind. Going back to Sheringham was not a possibility, nor, any longer, was going to her father – even though she now knew from reading with Will about herself on line, that he lived in Hexham rather than Norwich. She also now knew just how far Whittington Moor was from both Norfolk and Northumberland.

She felt fairly sure that successfully running away from Will would lead to her discovery and return to life with Milly, Jock and David. That was unthinkable. No, she'd stay and face the music – assuming there was any music to face. Maybe he hadn't seen her.

But maybe he had. And maybe he'd bumped into Harry as well, and Harry had told him about giving her the post. How was she going to explain that? She sat motionless at the kitchen table, staring at the fruit bowl, and waited for Will to come in.

She didn't have to wait long. And she could see immediately that she was in trouble. She bit her lip and watched as he pulled out the other chair and sat opposite her.

'I'm extremely disappointed in you Ariel.' He sounded cold and harsh. 'I thought I could trust you. I thought you wanted what I wanted and that we were in this together. Now I find out that you have been deceiving me for god knows how long, and worse: you've been talking to the postman about us. The postman for god's sake! There are probably no bigger gossips in England than postmen.' He was looking straight at her, holding her eyes with his and waiting for a response.

She didn't know what to say and thought quite probably she wouldn't be able to speak if she did know. She looked down at her hands, which were clenched tightly, so tightly it hurt.

'Well? And look at me, please.'

She squirmed, raised her eyes to about his chest height and, still unable to speak, wriggled a little and shrugged her shoulders. That was a mistake.

He banged his fist hard on the table, making her jump, and shouted, 'DAMMIT Ariel! Don't you know what you've done?'

She nodded miserably and found her voice. 'Shall I leave?'

'Oh don't be stupid. Bloody hell! I can't talk to you now. Go into your room – I'm going to lock the door so you can't get out and do any more damage. I can't be with you right now. I've got to think this through and see how we can repair the damage. If we can repair the damage. Go! I can't even look at you right now.'

He got up, angrily knocking over his chair, and waited for her to get up and go ahead of him up the stairs and into her room. He pulled the door shut with a bang behind her and, true to his word, she heard the key turn in the lock as she threw herself onto her bed and broke into body-wracking sobs.

•

He'd have to kill her. He'd done it before; he'd killed twice, on two separate occasions, and it had been quite easy. He'd heard it said that once you've committed a murder the first time, it's easy to do it again. He hadn't found it hard the first time – which had made him wonder about himself, occasionally. He didn't like the idea that he was a man without morals. Without empathy.

But he couldn't kill Ariel. He loved her. He hadn't loved the others – Sally Turp and Judith somebody-or-other, he'd forgotten. He hadn't even liked them very much at the start, and by the end he'd positively hated them. He'd picked up Sally outside a Travellers' camp in Somerset and regretted it every moment since. But he'd tried. He'd tried to indoctrinate her into being his Ariel, even though she wasn't interested and didn't have the intelligence to understand much of what he'd tried to teach her. She'd been blatantly rude to him when he tentatively broached the subject of their working together, as Will and Ariel Durant.

'That's what comes of picking up a Traveller,' he'd told himself, and set about ridding himself of the encumbrance and recovering his battered confidence.

He'd found Judith, a year later, even more bizarrely. She'd thumbed a lift from him in France and begged him to let her hide in the boot of his car to get across to England. She promised that if she were found she would not implicate him; she'd say he'd left the boot open and she'd just crawled in. Hoping she could be his next Ariel he'd agreed, and amazingly they'd got away with it. He'd seen nothing about her being missing – although English by birth, she'd lived all her life in France, so the British media had not really been much concerned. If there had been a hue and cry for her in France he hadn't known of it. As for Sally, nobody paid much attention to missing Travellers. There'd been a brief but mild flurry of interest in the media, followed quickly by total silence. Judith, too, had been useless as a life partner. She'd wanted the sex part, but would have nothing to do with knowledge or the Durants.

So, reluctantly, he'd killed them, each in their turn, nearly a year apart, as kindly as he could. He may have hated them, but he wasn't cruel. He'd waited until they slept, filled with alcohol supplied by him (though undoubtedly supplemented by more, stolen by them) then crept into the bedroom and held a pillow over their face until, after what had seemed to him a reasonably brief struggle, they'd been still. Disposing of them had been amazingly easy. Each time, he'd simply put the body into two large bin bags he'd taped together and then sewn the package into a thick duvet cover, securing the whole thing with duct tape. He'd put it in the boot of his car, driven to the north of Scotland, taken the ferry to Harris and Lewis and there, on the northernmost reaches of North Harris, had parked his car on a deserted cliff and bundled each one over the edge. No one saw him and on each occasion he was back on the mainland within four hours, home in Whittington Moor twelve hours after that. Until this year, as far as he knew, not a trace of either of them had washed up anywhere. And even then, he'd seen no reference to a connection having been made between either of them and the washed-up thigh bone. And for all he knew, there was no connection.

But he couldn't do that to Ariel. And yet he'd have to. There was no closing the Pandora's Box she'd opened by talking to the postman. Why had she done it? Did she hate him? Did she want him to end up in jail? Hadn't she sworn love for him, and declared that she wanted nothing more than to be Ariel to his Will Durant? What had changed her mind? Could it be as simple as youthful innocence on her part? He'd dearly love to believe that, but could he? And even if he could, what difference would it make?

He was desolate. It was the end of his dream; he could never do this again. In fact, if – no, when – he killed Ariel, he'd have to kill himself too. There was no point in going on.

They would die together then. They could die in each other's arms. If it had to happen – and it did – then at least it could happen well. Ariel and Will Durant had died within two weeks of each other; he and his Ariel would die within two minutes of each other.

TWENTY-ONE

Milly had been right about the probable lack of police reaction to the news that Jessie was actually a year older than they'd been led to believe. They half-heartedly pressed Milly to find out why, but she didn't seem to know, it just seemed to have happened that way when she was about five. She'd mistakenly told the school the child was four, and that had been that. At the time she hadn't been able to find Jessie's birth certificate and after two or three abortive requests, the school had given up asking. So four she was, for the record. And now as the police secretly – in reality, not so secretly – were convinced that the child had been dead for well over a year, they didn't think much action was called for. They did issue a press release that was carried deep in the middle of most papers and not at all by some. The photofit officer was assigned to produce an updated picture, but as no one thought a year's difference was all that important, it was not given a priority rating and so slipped further and further down the officer's to-do list.

Agnes mulled it over for a while, and brought it up to Les so often that he was forced to tell her to 'shut it'.

'Well I just can't help wondering why, that's all,' she'd said mutinously.

'Wonder all you like, but don't keep asking me to wonder with you. I couldn't care less.' And that, as far as Les was concerned, was that. His luscious whitening leeks were far more worthy of his attention. There wasn't room in his mind for much else. With the possible exception, late at night, of what it might be like to bed Milly.

•

By early evening Will had worn himself out pacing, crying, fuming, fretting, planning and despairing. He still wasn't thinking clearly, he was aware of that, but he knew he needed to cut off the angst and try, at least, to think straight and rationally.

He'd half-heard Ariel crying on and off all day, but for the moment she was quiet. He'd hardened his heart to her sobbing so far, but now he suddenly felt a rush of horror at the thought of her lying there, desolate, abandoned and afraid. What sort of a beast was he? He claimed to love her and want the best for her, but this was the second – no, third – time he'd been oblivious to her pain. Even if he was going to kill her – and he was no longer so sure – he should have some empathy for her suffering.

He dug into the back of his liquor cabinet and found a bottle of Scotch whisky. Then, remembering where he'd bought it, put it back and reached for the cognac instead. He was not really a drinking man, but felt he really needed a little comfort now. Brandy for medicinal purposes he said to himself wryly and poured himself a fairly stiff tot.

He sipped it as he fed the two cats and made himself some toast, more than half of which he couldn't eat. He thought about having another Cognac, but decided against it. Alcohol was not the route to clear thinking.

On the kitchen table was last Saturday's jumbo cryptic crossword, some squares filled in by Ariel in her careful, neat, but still quite childish, letters. Most answers were scrawled in his own spidery hand. The pain he felt, looking at their shared effort and remembering the utter contentment of so many hours of such activities, almost bent him double. He sat down quickly and pushed the newspaper away.

'So what would I like? What would comfort me now?' he heard himself say out loud. He picked up one of the cats – Ethel, he thought – but she was having none of it. In the first place she wanted her food and in the second she had bonded to Louis more than to the humans. She was available for cuddling on her terms only. That was no help, Will thought.

'What can I do?' he asked the cat as he put her back down. He watched her walk over and nuzzle Louis, and knew the answer immediately. Sleep. But not just ordinary sleep. Sleep wrapped around his love, his Ariel, just as Ethel would soon sleep cuddled up to Louis, that's what would comfort him.

•

There was no sound at all from her room as he unlocked the door and went in as quietly as he could. In the half-darkness he could see Ariel, still in the clothes she'd had on that morning, sprawled sideways across the bed, sleeping. Her face was puffy and tear-stained and, as he watched, her chest convulsed slightly as if she were still sobbing. He pulled off his jumper and jogging bottoms and slowly eased himself onto the bed beside her, wrapping himself around her body, his front pressed to her back.

Oh the relief! The comfort flooded his whole being. He could breathe again. He matched his breathing to hers, breathing in on her intake and out on her expiration. If they were to die like this – but not now – it would be fine. He could live with that. He gave a small snort and shook his head a little as he realised what he'd just said to himself. The movement disturbed her and she shifted her position a little.

'It's all right, my love, it's all right. I'm here,' he murmured into her hair.

She tried to pull herself out of his arms but he held her close to him.

'It's really all right, just stay where you are and it will all be fine, I promise you.'

'I'm sorry Will. I really, really am...' she seemed about to cry again and he knew he couldn't bear that.

'Shush. Shush. I know you are. It's okay. It's really okay. We've got each other and that's all that matters tonight.' He rocked her gently as he held her. 'Sleep now. I'll be here and we'll sleep together tonight, and tomorrow we'll work out what to do next. It will be all right.'

'Really? Will it really be all right?'

'Yes. I don't know quite how yet, but it will. Now sleep.'

She did as she was told almost instantly. He didn't stay awake himself for long, just long enough to think, 'I don't know how but it must be all right. How could something that feels so right not work out?'

•

When she woke up in the bright morning light she was under the covers, still in Will's arms. He must have moved them into the bed during the night then. She liked having him wrapped around her; she wished the moment could last forever.

He was awake. 'Hello life partner,' he said softly. 'How do you feel this morning?'

How did she feel? Drained, frightened, ashamed, sick, but strangely peaceful, as long as she could stay where she was.

'All right,' was all she said, flatly.

'Stay here a little longer. I'll make us some tea and then we'll talk.' He slid out of bed and pulled on his jogging bottoms and jumper. Ariel felt a little shudder of shock when she heard him lock the door behind him. He still didn't trust her. But then, why should he? How could he, after what she'd done?

She went to the bathroom, had a quick wash, cleaned her teeth and put on some clean clothes. She never wanted to see yesterday's clothes again, so bundled them into the cupboard, behind one of the cardboard boxes labelled A-II. She would like to forget yesterday. Perhaps Will would teach her how. He seemed to be good at forgetting things he didn't like remembering, like his real name and what his cousin had died of. She wondered again how he did it. It was good to have something like that to think about so she didn't keep remembering the awfulness of yesterday.

There was something she had forgotten though. Crikey! Today was the day the man from the BTO was coming to see the hoopoe! She'd been working up to telling Will about that, hoping he'd be pleased at her independence and not angry that she'd phoned them again without asking. She'd thought briefly if she should ask, but had enjoyed a small urge to be defiant and had then rationalised that he'd been all right about her phoning them before and describing the bird and getting their genuine interest in it. She hadn't really expected anyone to want to come and see for themselves, but as she saw the bird most days on her early morning walk, the BTO man had said he would come today and if he had no luck he would try again tomorrow. He came from Norfolk, he'd said, but had to be in Birmingham for a conference this week, so a morning run out to Whittington Moor would be a pleasure. She hadn't known how to direct him here but he'd asked for the postcode and found the house immediately on something he called his satnav. She didn't know what that was, but was relieved that he would know how to find her.

She wondered what it would be like to see a man who came from Norfolk. Would he be able to tell that she'd come from Norfolk, over a year ago? She didn't see how he could, but she wasn't sure. What she was sure of was that she couldn't ask Will. She'd better not even tell him. Perhaps the man – Dave – would come and look and then go away again, and no one would be any the wiser. She didn't see how she was going to be out there anyway, as Will had locked her in the bedroom. She hoped he wasn't going to leave her there alone all day again.

•

As usual, things looked a lot less black now that he'd had a good night's sleep. And no bad dream. Far from it, he'd mixed his dreams with his waking reality and had been snuggled up to Ariel all night long in both. He actually felt quite cheerful this morning.

After a quick shower and shave he fed the cats and turned on the computer as he waited for the kettle to boil. He had been in the habit of regularly Googling 'Jessie Pike' in the early days, but had not done so lately. The cookie was still active though, and up popped a reference in one of the tabloid newspapers, referring to the press release from the Norfolk Constabulary about her age. She was, it said, a year older than they'd been led to believe. He could hardly believe his eyes. She was thirteen then, not twelve. How? Why? But did it make any real difference?

Well, it meant she could kiss him on the mouth in less than a year – if she still wanted to. It also meant they were one year closer to being able to get married legally. He Googled Marriages in Scotland to see just how long he had to wait and what documents they'd need. The first web site he got to was quite encouraging. Ariel would have to be sixteen (but that was better than eighteen, as she'd have to be in England to marry without her parents' consent) and whilst it would be helpful if they could produce a birth certificate, it didn't seem to be mandatory. Other documents showing her age would apparently do. He wasn't sure of the route to getting other documents, but he felt it might be possible, in the three years they had to wait, to start with something simple, like a Tesco loyalty card, a library card, and keep moving up until she possessed something more likely to be taken as gospel by a marriage registrar. Three months' notice of the wedding was required: so no problem there, he thought, they could have three years' notice if they liked. And you didn't have to be resident in Scotland; in fact you didn't seem to have to prove anything about where you live. Two witnesses were needed but several subsequent 'wedding' sites guaranteed to provide them for you.

He felt better. If he wasn't going to have to produce an authentic birth document, what was to stop them moving her up by a year – or even two? Right now, of course, she wouldn't pass for sixteen, but next year she might and certainly she would by the time she was fifteen. He felt better still and Googled frivolously for ten minutes or so before taking the tea back to Ariel's bedroom.

•

Her heart felt as if it turned over in her chest when she heard Will unlock the door, but he was smiling as he came in.

'Here we are, tea to draw us together as they say.' He handed her a mug and sat down on the bed with his. 'You look fresher. Do you feel up to talking now?'

He seemed more like his usual kind self, much to her relief. She didn't know what she was supposed to be saying, but she was certainly willing to cooperate in any way he liked. She nodded vigorously to demonstrate that willingness.

'It's really all about damage control now. And at the moment it's impossible to say what the extent of the damage is. Can you be really truthful with me now, do you think, and tell me exactly everything you have told the postman? Even if you think it isn't important?'

That would be easy. 'Oh yes, Will. And I haven't talked to him very much. I met him accidentally one morning when I was out looking at the birds. And then it just seemed to work out that I was out there when he came. He wanted to give me the post but I didn't want to bring it in to you so I always left it in the box.'

'Except for the day you shoved it under a bush halfway

down the drive. What happened that day?'

'That was on my birthday. It... I was... I think I was so excited about it being my birthday that I forgot.' She couldn't look at him now that she wasn't quite telling the truth.

'Did you tell him it was your birthday?'

She couldn't answer. Her heart began pounding again.

'Did you?' Silence. 'You did, didn't you? Ariel – you must tell me. If I don't know it all, then there's no hope of our getting out of this. It's done now; I'm not going to scold you about it – well not much – I'm certainly not going to shout at you. But I must know. Did you tell him?'

'Yes,' miserably. Then, 'I told him you are my dad, too.'

He took a deep breath. 'Did you tell him you'd come from Sheringham and that I'd picked you up – or anything like that? Anything about how we met? The truth now, Ariel. I must have the truth.'

She was relieved to be able to answer honestly on this one. 'On my honour, no, Will. I told him you are my dad and that I live with you and that it was my birthday. I was twelve.' She looked at his eyes and thought, irrelevantly, what a nice colour they were. A sort of milk-chocolate brownish tan. Like the insides of Maltesers.

'That's all. The other days we just talked about birds. Oh, and he said he knew about everybody from delivering their post. I think he reads their postcards,' she dropped her voice, a little ashamed of her friend Harry.

'Well he won't get any joy there about us.' Will seemed to be relaxing a little, so she relaxed a little too. Perhaps she wouldn't mention the BTO man and get him upset again. For the first time she hoped and prayed the hoopoe wouldn't be out there, so if Dave came, he'd get nothing and would leave again quickly. If Will ever let her out of the bedroom she might sneak in a phone call to Dave's BTO office and ask them to tell him not to come at all, that she'd made a big mistake and it was just an ordinary jay. If Will ever let her out of her bedroom.

•

119

'A red tick on the calendar this morning,' he said, now willing to change the subject. 'They just popped out into my hand as nice as you like.'

'Great. Any black cross?' She knew the significance of the black cross.

'No. No black cross this morning, thank heavens.' He opened the cupboard door and surveyed the boxes. 'I hadn't realised these were still here. We need to get rid of them.' He moved two boxes then picked up the bundle of her yesterday's clothes and frowned. 'Please don't just toss your laundry into the cupboard, Ariel. You've a perfectly good laundry basket in your bathroom.' He held them out to her. She meekly took them into the bathroom and deposited them in the wicker basket. He recognised that she was annoyed with herself for her carelessness and realised that she was working hard to get back in his good books. He couldn't decide if that felt good to him or simply made him feel uncomfortable.

'What's in the boxes, Will?'

'Nothing important – things I thought I might need again but I won't. We'll put them in the boot of the car and drop them off somewhere on our way.'

'On our way where? Where are we going?'

'I'm not sure yet, but I think we need to go away for a few days. I'm thinking about Scotland. It's nice and peaceful up there. One of the northern islands like Skye, or Harris and Lewis. What do you think, Ariel?'

'What about Ethel and Louis? Will they be able to come?'

'Oh. No, I don't think so. No,' firmly, 'I'll ask Mrs Leeds if she'll take care of them until we're back. She'll treat them well and take very good care of them.' He knew the cats were important to Ariel, even if she did leave most of their daily care to him. It might be risky to reveal their going away to Mrs Leeds, but he was prepared to risk it. He needed Ariel's cooperation. 'I'll take them down there this evening. I won't take you with me of course. You'll stay here.'

'Locked in?'

'Yes.' Giving Ariel access to outside or the telephone at this stage was a risk he wasn't prepared to take. 'I have to learn to trust you again, Ariel. You have to earn that trust.'

She drooped but said nothing.

'Don't look so melancholy. I'm sure you'll be trustworthy again very quickly. Meantime I'm not letting you out of my sight unless you are safely locked in here. There are consequences for our behaviours you know. That's something worth remembering.'

•

They'd spent most of the day packing. Ariel was half excited and half dead scared, but managed to do as she was told and be helpful. Will didn't seem to be in the best of moods, but some of the time all seemed normal and he talked about the Durants or Walt Whitman, or a clue from the crossword. She'd had a panic when he found a note in the door signed 'Dave', saying 'Knocked a few times but evidently nobody home. Will try again tomorrow.' She decided to be as mystified as Will was as to its origin. She'd worry about tomorrow, tomorrow. She was getting pretty good at that.

In the event she didn't have to. When it got dark he locked her in the bedroom again and said he was taking the cats to Mrs Leeds, who had, he said, agreed to take good care of them. Ariel had found it difficult to say goodbye to them, but knew it was her fault that they were leaving, so tried to keep her tears in check until she'd heard Will drive away.

When he came back he was, he said, 'ready to roll'. They loaded the car with the last-minute items, including Will's computer – 'Can't be without that!' – then followed each other around the house making sure taps and lights were all turned off. Even though Will had said were only going for a few days, she feared they would not be coming back here. This feeling was heightened when he pulled her close to him for a hug in the hallway.

'We've had some pretty good times here, haven't we Ariel?' He wiped her tears gently with the handkerchief she had liked the best – the dark blue checked one. 'But don't worry, we'll have lots more good times in Scotland. We have our whole life ahead of us.'

TWENTY-TWO

Dave had not been surprised not to find a hoopoe. He'd lost count of the number of false alarms he'd covered – wild goose chases, he liked to say – but he'd been perfectly truthful when he told Ariel that he would enjoy a quick run out to the countryside after spending all the day before in Birmingham. In many respects he was quite glad of the opportunity to do it all again next morning. 'You never know,' he said to himself for the umpteenth time in his career. 'You just never know.'

He had been a bit surprised to find that there was apparently no one home though. There was a car in the driveway and a light on in one of the upstairs rooms. It wasn't that early, he thought, and the woman had surely been expecting him. She'd sounded nice – young. He'd been looking forward to meeting her. Ariel, she'd said her name was, Ariel Pike. 'Ariel's a nice name for a birdwatcher,' he'd said. 'And Pike – are you a fisherperson as well?' She'd giggled and he'd thought what a nice giggle she had. He'd definitely been looking forward to meeting her.

He'd come back tomorrow if he could. If not, before the end of the week.

•

They headed north, stopping in Stoke-on-Trent and then in Warrington to leave the boxes from Ariel's cupboard outside Oxfam, Sue Ryder and Cancer Research charity shops. It was close to midnight when they left the motorway to find a hotel for the night on the edge of the Lake District. Ariel was barely awake, so he locked her in the car while he went in to register – as Mr and Mrs Wills, paying cash and counting on the fact that the weary-looking woman at reception wouldn't pay any attention to them. He felt what he was sure must be a visible tingle as he answered her 'Twin or double, sir?' with a casual, 'Double, please.'

He went back to the car and got the two suitcases they'd packed for overnight and, locking her in once more, took the luggage and his computer up to their room. Then he went back, put the car in its proper slot in the car park, woke Ariel and, with a supporting arm around her middle, walked with her back up to their room.

'Are we in Scotland?' she asked sleepily.

'Not yet. We're in the Lake District. I'll show you on the map. Tomorrow we'll become tourists for the day and have a good look round. We might even take a boat out on one of the lakes. Would you like that?'

'Umm,' she said, 'not too early though.'

He smiled. 'No. Look, there's the bathroom – go and wash your face and clean your teeth and get undressed for bed. You can have a bath in the morning.' He didn't point out that they were to share a bed. Perhaps she wouldn't comment, perhaps it would just happen seamlessly. He thought he would have a bath once she was in bed and that she would then most likely be deeply asleep by the time he got in.

She wasn't long, emerging from the bathroom already in her pyjamas and climbing into bed with a sigh. 'Nice,' she said, and snuggled down into the pillow.

'I'll have a quick bath now. And say goodnight in case you are asleep when I've finished.' He leaned over and kissed her forehead. They had been in the habit of having a goodnight hug for many months now, but this was the first time he had actually kissed her. Openly, at least. He'd occasionally dropped a light kiss on her hair when they'd hugged.

He lay in the bath for a long time. He was looking forward to getting into bed with Ariel but thought he'd better take care of his urgent physical needs first. Besides, delaying the pleasure only heightened it. He decided they would never again sleep in separate beds, married or not.

The epiphany hit him like an electric shock. In a flash the idea, almost fully formed, filled his mind and he lay there in wonder. Of course! How stupid he'd been.

He got out of the bath and hastily dried himself and pulled on a clean t-shirt and boxer shorts. Should he rouse Ariel and tell her his revelation, the new plan? No. It wouldn't be kind to wake her, and besides, the anticipation of her relief would only increase that pleasure too. He hadn't told her she was actually thirteen yet, either. And would therefore – another frisson tore through him like an electric charge – have only less than a year, not two, to wait before she could kiss him on the mouth.

'Whoa, whoa!' He sat on the edge of the bath and took a deep breath. He mustn't get carried away. She was still only thirteen and much as he physically desired her now, it was too soon to be thinking about that aspect of their future together. Never mind the fact that a sexual relationship with her now would be illegal. He smiled bitterly at himself. He was a murderer and didn't care, but the idea of committing statutory rape was a step too far, even for him. Well, that's what love could do for you, he thought. My love for Ariel and hers for me is making me a better person.

He looked in the mirror. Should he shave? 'Nah, this isn't your wedding night, Archimedes!' He smiled again but this time with genuine happiness. Tomorrow he'd enjoy telling Ariel the Archimedes and his eureka moment-in-his-bath story, too, and he knew she would enjoy the image of the ancient philosopher running naked through the streets of Syracuse. He cleaned his teeth, splashed on some aftershave for the smell of it and went quietly into the bedroom.

•

She wasn't asleep when Will came in. She'd dozed a lot on the journey so was able to keep herself awake now, wondering if he was going to sleep with her again that night. If not, she couldn't think where he would sleep; she was pretty sure they only had the one room. Did she dare hope? And could she say anything if he didn't get into bed with her? She felt very much on her best behaviour, a great need to make amends and earn Will's trust again. She was anxious not to do anything that might rock the boat between them.

'Not asleep?' He was in his underwear, she could see that in the dim light. And he was going to sleep with her – he got in beside her. 'Shall we cuddle again?'

'Please. I liked that, Will.'

'Then you may be pleased to know that from now on we'll sleep together always. Is that all right with you?'

'Oh yes.' She snuggled against him, inhaling his clean soapy smell mixed with his aftershave. This was paradise! And they were going to do it every night. She could hardly believe it – and after all she'd done to betray him, too.

'I'm rather glad you're awake. I had a wonderful realisation in the bath. I'm not going to tell you about it tonight but I'm happy to be able to tell you with great confidence that it's going to be all right – I've worked out how we're going to carry on. So you can go to sleep, my divinely terrible girl, knowing that all will be well.'

'I could sleep better if I knew you could forgive me, Will.' For all his niceness and excitement and loving cuddling, she couldn't tell if he was still, underneath, angry and disappointed with her.

'Sweet child, of course I forgive you. And I understand. Will Durant believed that forgiveness and understanding are the two halves of philosophy, so I can do no less. I don't forgive and forget though – it's more like forgive and remember, so I don't get caught out again. But I'm not holding a grudge. You are forgiven. There.' And he kissed her forehead again.

'Goodnight then, Will.' She relaxed against him and immediately fell asleep.

•

Lying next to Ariel in bed, Will thought about his face as he'd seen it in the bathroom mirror. Should he grow a beard? Would it make him look younger or older? It could be a bit of a disguise but actually, if his current plan worked, he wouldn't need a disguise. So he'd ask Ariel at some point if she'd like him to grow a beard. Not a moustache though, at least not by itself. He was too young for that. That would be for when he was older; he could start smoking a pipe then, too. And Ariel, sweetly plump and contented in her middle age would put his slippers by the fire to warm… He sighed with his own contented pleasure and drifted into a deep and dreamless sleep.

•

'I've been thinking about our future in the wrong way, Ariel.' They were up, having room service breakfast and both eager to

126

talk about Will's 'epiphany' of the night before.

'I've been wondering how to hide you until you can legally become my wife – especially now that people in Whittington know of your existence. And unfortunately, you've told them you are my daughter.'

'I only told the postman, Will.'

'Yes, well, as I told you, that's tantamount to putting a notice in the paper, on the radio and hiring a sky writer to announce it, but never mind. We'll rise above it. It no longer matters anyway. We are leaving Whittington Moor and moving somewhere entirely new to live – where we will live as man and wife. We will become Mr and Mrs Dee without having to go through a ceremony. It won't really matter if we never actually legally marry. We would just go on living together, in free love, and eventually we'd become what they call 'common-law' husband and wife and then I think we'd be the same as legally married. I'll have to find out if that's still true. How do you feel about that?'

She honestly didn't know, and spoke without thinking. 'Does that mean you can't be my dad any more?'

She could see he struggled to be patient.

'Ariel, I was never your dad. And I never can be your dad. That was a fantasy you created – and if I may say so, it's done nothing but cause us trouble. No, my plan has always been for you to be my wife, just like Ariel married Will Durant. They worked on their life project together and that's what we are going to do.'

'She was fourteen, though. I'm only twelve.' Being Will's wife one day felt maybe all right to her, but she didn't know if she was up to it yet. Could she somehow be his daughter and his wife, she wondered, but didn't dare say anything.

'Ah, that's the other lovely piece of news. You are actually thirteen – you'll soon be fourteen, legally next March, even though we won't celebrate it until May.'

She was confused. 'How can I be thirteen now? I'm only twelve.'

'No, we thought you were twelve, we assumed you were twelve. But yesterday, before we left, I found a small press release online saying that your actual birth certificate had been found and it revealed that you are actually a year older than your mother had been telling you. And don't ask me why – I cannot imagine. Unless she wasn't married and wanted to pretend you weren't born until after she'd married your dad. Though these days people really don't worry about that anymore. But anyway, you are thirteen, a young lady, not a child. And I love you!'

Ariel struggled to comprehend what it all meant – and how their life might change if they adopted this new relationship. But as he so often did, Will seemed to read her thoughts.

'Nothing will change for a while though, so please don't worry about it. Yes, we'll share a bed, but I'm not going to "demand my marital rights" if that's what's worrying you.'

Not knowing what that meant, Ariel shook her head. 'No. It's not. But where are we going to live? And can we have Ethel and Louis with us?'

'I don't know where yet. All I know is that we'll sell the Whittington Moor house and move somewhere where nobody knows us and we'll move there as Mr and Mrs Dee. I'll see if we can get the cats back though. Meantime, we're having a little holiday in Scotland before we go back to the Moor to pack it all up. I'm wildly excited, Ariel. And so relieved; I can't think why I didn't think of this before. I had an epiphany in the bath last night – an Archimedes-eureka moment, you might say.'

She looked at him quizzically and began to feel much safer and more relaxed as he assumed the familiar role of teacher and explained to her what that meant. 'He might not see himself as my dad,' she thought with face-crinkling determination and her mouth in a straight, stubborn line, 'but I still do.'

128

TWENTY-THREE

'Bill says the Dee girl doesn't go to his school,' Mrs Leeds told Mrs Simmons on the following Tuesday. 'But he's willing to go out to the house to see if it's all right and proper, he says.'

Mrs Simmons tried not to show she was thrilled. 'Ooh, I think that's a very good idea,' she cooed. 'Best to be sure. It would be awful if we did nothing and then found out there was something going on that shouldn't be.'

'Oh I don't think there'll be anything like that, Mrs S,' Mrs Leeds didn't share the postmistress's dark turn of mind. 'But as you say, best to be sure.'

Mrs Simmons knew that telling Harry would be more rewarding. Harry had an abiding interest in all his 'patrons', as he referred to them. And thoroughly enjoyed passing on titbits about their personal lives, usually gleaned from their post, to Mrs Simmons. She, naturally enough, was deeply interested and was a most encouraging audience. And sure enough, Harry got right into it. 'What's he going to say then, our Mr Leeds?'

'I expect he'll ask if she's going to another school. I don't think he can ask if she's having underage sex – can he?'

'I don't think he can ask anything at the moment. They ain't there. I've put today's post on top of yesterday's, such as it is. He'll have a wasted journey if he goes out now.'

'I'll tell him then. I'll give them a ring and tell them what you said. Then you can tell me when they're back so Bill Leeds can go out and see.'

'Hokey-dokey. Wonder where they've gone, though.'

•

Dave had not been able to revisit Whittington Moor on the next morning but, because of commitments at his conference, had been forced to wait a couple of days. It didn't matter though; he was luckier on his second visit. There was the hoopoe, bold as brass with its long curved bill poking about for insects and its crest wiggling in the breeze as it pecked its way across the scrubby grass. With years of practice, Dave quickly pulled out his camera with the telephoto lens and got several perfect shots of the bird before it realised Dave was watching – at which point it took off, somewhat more gracefully than he'd have expected, and looking rather like an enormous monochrome butterfly.

'Bingo!' he said. He'd never lost the thrill of seeing something unexpected or in an unexpected place. He spent several minutes documenting the details in his official blue notebook and then went to the front door and knocked. There was no car in the drive this morning, no lights anywhere and no answer to his knock. Somehow the house seemed unoccupied, though he could not have said why he felt that.

He walked slowly back up the drive and was about to get into his car when the post van pulled up alongside him. The postman rolled down his window and stuck out his head. 'Morning, squire. Nasty corner this. Any sign of anybody in this morning?'

Dave shook his head. 'Nope. Shame really, I'd like to tell them that the lady was right about seeing the hoopoe. That's an unusual bird in these parts,' he added; he could see the postman was not a birdwatcher. 'Mrs Pike was so excited, I'd like to see her face when I tell her she was right.'

'Mrs Pike? Who's that then? There's a Mr Dee what lives here. Him and his young teenage daughter. Ariel, her name is.'

'Oh, Ariel Pike, that would be his daughter then. I see.' Dave was vaguely disappointed. He'd thought the woman was older.

'Well, that's what she told me, anyway. Ariel Dee though, not Ariel Pike. Well, I must be getting on. I just wondered if they was back home yet. Ta-rah.'

•

Mrs. Simmons was bursting with news. She could hardly wait for Harry to take his coat off before she launched in.

'Well! You'll never guess. They've gone away!'

'I know. I told you,' Harry was unmoved. This wasn't news.

'Ah, but you didn't know it was for permanent, did you?'

130

Fair do's. He hadn't known that.

'How do you know it is?'

This was just the opening she was waiting for. She took a deep breath and seemed to swell up in front of him.

'Mrs Leeds told me. She found them two cats in a box on her doorstep with a note saying he had to be away for a while so would she please have them back. People don't do that if they're just going away for the weekend. Or even a fortnight. There!' She set her mouth in a straight line and nodded vigorously. 'And he didn't say "we" either, he said "I". No mention of the girl.'

'So much for old Bill Leeds going up there to find out about her then. Now we'll never know I suppose.' Harry was disappointed. 'What am I to do with his post, Mrs S?'

'Well, we haven't had any official notification or request to hold it. You'll have to go on putting it in the box I suppose. Though you could leave a note saying the box is full so we're holding it at the post office… yes, I like that idea, then he'd have to come in to get it. Here, I'll write the note for you.'

'Righty-ho. I'll take it up tomorrow. Oh, I bumped into a man from some bird watching thing up there this morning. Said he was looking for hoo-poo-somethings.'

'That'll be whooping cranes, I daresay,' Mrs Simmons watched all the nature programmes and liked to think she was an expert on wildlife too.

'Maybe. Anyway, he was looking for a Mrs Pike – seemed right surprised when I said it was the Dees what live there.'

'Mrs Pike? There's no Mrs Pike round these parts. Probably no whooping cranes neither.'

TWENTY-FOUR

They'd spent the day in Kendall and decided to stay in the same hotel for a second night. Will kept looking at Ariel, trying to see how others might perceive her. Reluctantly he concluded that they were more likely to see her as his daughter than his wife or girlfriend, but he couldn't for the moment see what he could do about that. Get her some different clothes maybe? A different hairstyle? He did take her hand and hold it everywhere they walked, trying to look husbandly, rather than paternal.

Actually, he realised, nobody is really looking at us anyway. So should they be looking for a place to live that was like this – rather than something out in the country as he'd had at Whittington Moor? Hiding in plain sight was always said to be more effective than trying to bury yourself in the country where people noticed – and commented on – everything. Except, he reminded himself gleefully, they didn't need to hide. They wanted people to see them and take them as husband and wife, a couple who had moved here – wherever it turned out to be – from somewhere else. Somerset, he'd say. He was familiar enough with the Quantock Hills area to be able to bluff his way through about having lived there. In fact, he had lived there, briefly, as a child, before his parents had moved back to the Tamworth area and at an earlier point he had done not a small amount of online research on the area as a possible place for himself to live one day.

There was such a lot to think about. He needed a short holiday, away from the gossips and possible danger of Whittington Moor, and with the opportunity to think and plan in careful detail. He didn't know how he was going to get the blasted cats back, but he hadn't the heart to deny Ariel that. At least, not immediately. Besides, as she'd said 'They're our children.' He'd think of something. Maybe he'd say they were happier with Mrs Leeds, though he couldn't imagine her believing that for a moment. And that would be a bad start to their new relationship and life together. No, he'd have to think up a way to approach Mrs Leeds and take them back, claiming a misunderstanding if she'd thought – as well she might – that he was giving them back to her for good. Yes, he'd do that, pretending they were back at Whittington Moor and then they'd quietly pack up everything and move to parts unknown. No forwarding address; he never got anything important through the post anyway. He did all his business online and he could be anywhere in the world for that.

They'd hire a moving company from Birmingham; not a big company, he'd look in the Yellow Pages and get one that would, for cash, be tight-lipped if necessary, and keep no records. He could sell his car and buy something second hand, privately, and under an assumed name if he could, but he didn't think he needed to. No one was actually looking for him. He kept reminding himself of that. He'd close up the house and sell it online or give it to a property management company to handle. Yet again he reassured himself, he could do that with impunity because nobody was looking for him. They might have been, if he and Ariel had continued living at Whittington Moor, but he felt reasonably sure they were not the object of anything other than mild village curiosity at the moment.

He hadn't discussed any of this with Ariel. He hadn't felt the need to. When she, apparently concerned over his feelings about leaving, had asked, 'Have you lived at Whittington Moor for a long time, Will?' he'd responded: 'The time before you came doesn't have any relevance to me now. And in fact, this house isn't important to me. You are the important thing; well, us. I shan't mind leaving here because wherever we are I shall be with you.' And he'd meant it.

•

Dave always went over to his sister and brother-in-law's house for Bonfire Night. They had young children and the little kid in Dave enjoyed letting off fireworks with them and roasting spuds and chestnuts in the bonfire. He envied his sister her married status and wondered whether if he'd done as she had and joined the police force, he might have met somebody he could settle down with. The sort of birding job he did was quite isolated really. Janice and Roger were always very welcoming so he went often. As a result, they knew a lot about his job – which was also his passion.

'Seen anything exciting lately, Dave?' Roger popped the top

off the beer bottle and handed it to his brother-in-law.

'Nothing at all since the hoopoe this summer.'

'Yes. That was a rum go wasn't it? Did you ever make contact with the people that had phoned you?'

'No. They never answered the phone and they never responded to my letter. Shame really. The lady was really excited and I wanted to tell her that it had been verified. I don't know if she'll see it in our mag. I put it in anyway, not quite giving the exact location since I hadn't got their permission, but I did give her credit. Ariel Pike. I liked her name, that's why.'

Roger swallowed his beer and frowned. 'Ariel who? Pike? That was the name of that girl that went missing from Sheringham – oh, nearly two years ago, wasn't it? Janice! What was the name of that girl that went missing from Sheringham?'

'I can't remember. Jennifer? No, wait, Jessica something?'

'No, not Jessica, but something like it. Jessie! Jessie Pike, wasn't it?'

'Could have been. Why?'

'Probably nothing in it, but Dave's missing hoopoe woman was named Ariel Pike. My copper's nose is twitching, that's all. They never found her, did they?'

'I honestly can't remember Rog. Why don't you ring the station and ask if they still have a man on it if you're interested. Meanwhile please make yourself useful and light some more sparklers for the kids.'

'I might do that. Like I say, my nose is itching.'

TWENTY-FIVE

'Have you ever celebrated your birthday in Scotland before, Will?' Ariel was relishing her role as housewife in the small cottage they'd rented near Lusta on the west coast of Skye. Today she had made scones, cheese straws, chocolate cupcakes and some kind of casserole to use up as much of their food as she could. This was to be their last few days there before returning to Whittington Moor to carry out Will's plan to close up and sell the house. Will had put it on the market online and there were already several people interested in looking at it. He wanted to get all their stuff out of there and hand over the keys to the agent before that happened.

'I'm sure I haven't. And in any case, no celebrations that took place before you joined my life have any meaning at all.' He was so happy that he often forgot the scare that had brought them here. When he did remember, he had to remind himself that he was not a fugitive from the law and therefore had no real need to cover his tracks. It was just his nature to be secretive.

Sleeping with Ariel – in the literal sense of the phrase only – was one of his greatest pleasures and comforts. So much so that he had not had a single nightmare since before their first night together. He kept telling himself that he must wait until she was fourteen – next March, actually, though they wouldn't celebrate it until May – but he could easily imagine himself making love to her in whatever their new home turned out to be. He told himself he was working up to it gradually; caressing her sleepily compliant body in bed, cupping her small but perfect breasts in his hand. Once, when he was sure she was asleep, he had pushed up her pyjama top and put his mouth on her nipple briefly. She had mumbled and shifted so he withdrew quickly. He did not want to alarm her or give her anything other than a blissfully glorious experience, so was willing to go as slowly as necessary. She occasionally brought up the half-promised kiss on the mouth that was supposed to happen at fourteen. She had begun dropping hints about 'something special' for his birthday, and he had drifted into believing it was going to happen today. That would be fine with him, especially as the impetus would be coming from her. Just like the original Ariel and Will, he thought exultantly.

They were both more casual with each other, neither of them locking the bathroom door and neither of them being anything other than nonchalant if the other walked in during bath time. The first time he'd seen her pubic hair he could hardly stop himself crowing with delight; it was such a wonderfully deep rich auburn colour. For several nights afterwards he'd had rich and graphic dreams, and was profoundly grateful that Ariel slept so deeply that she wasn't disturbed by his half-muffled moans.

•

Ariel knew she was being coquettish and she was enjoying it, even though she had no idea the word existed. She wasn't consciously retaliating for Will's delaying of her 'main present'; that was too long ago. Another lifetime, before she was Ariel. But it was fun to tease him, hinting that she might be giving him something special for his birthday, and that that something might be the promised kiss on the lips, even if she wasn't yet fourteen. Will had delayed two of her birthdays by two months each, she reasoned, so it seemed only fair for her to bring forward the most important thing about her next birthday by a few months to make up for it. She liked the symmetry of the numbers.

The prospect excited her. She would sometimes look at his face and imagine how it would feel to have her lips against his, and wondered if her namesake had actually planned the event or whether it had been completely spontaneous. She herself favoured the spontaneous approach, but knew that she had thought about it for so long that it was never going to be that. So she gave herself over to the pleasure of planning. She had learned that the funny feeling in the pit of her belly had nothing to do with her period, but had a lot to do with thinking about, enjoying – and wanting more – physical contact with Will. She wasn't sure of the mechanics of these things, though she felt sure Will would know, and she was feeling more and more ready to experiment and find out.

Delayed gratification was as yet another unknown phrase to her, but the concept in this instance had appeal. She had decided to give him other presents today, his birthday, and save the kiss a little longer; until they moved into their new home. That would be a week or two from now and she thought she could wait that long – indeed, she would enjoy the wait and the anticipation. Will had said plenty of times that anticipation is the best part of the event, and she was beginning to think he might be onto something. Perhaps not the 'best' part though; she hoped – and believed – the actual event would at least equal the anticipation.

Buying him presents had not been easy. For one thing, it was hard to get him to leave her alone in a shop but she had managed to get a cut glass vase he'd admired in the gift shop at the Talisker Distillery whilst he was sampling the whisky. She'd also found – and bought without his noticing – a book of The Times cryptic crosswords in a bookshop in Portree, and she'd made him a montage of photographs of the Durants that she had scanned and printed on his computer when he thought she was playing Hearts and spider solitaire. To her intense relief his persistent surveillance of her had lessened considerably over the weeks they had been at Lusta.

Ariel had mixed feelings about moving, not fully understanding why it was necessary but, as always, feeling that as long as she was with Will – and not in Sheringham – it wouldn't matter where they were. She'd smiled when he told her that Ariel Durant's grandfather had moved his family because he had seen a woman in the house opposite with her arms bared to the elbows. At least Will's reason for their move – whatever it was – wasn't that silly.

They were moving to Gloucester. Will had taken a lease with option to buy on a cottage on the edge of the city and they were to live there ostensibly as husband and wife – as they had been doing on Skye. Not that it mattered here; nobody took the slightest bit of notice of them anyway. But Will rarely missed an opportunity to refer to her as his wife in shops or cafes. She hadn't been able to say 'my husband' yet, but she'd been practising under her breath, whilst wishing she could be saying 'dad'. Sometimes she amused herself with the idea that, as her dad, he could give permission for her to marry him – as her husband. She didn't share this fantasy with Will. And – quite new to her – she knew why she didn't.

They would be leaving the day after tomorrow, Will had said. They would drive down to the Midlands, taking their time and staying somewhere overnight – two or three nights if they felt like it. Once back at Whittington Moor they would pack up everything for the movers – who were booked to come early next week – collect Ethel and Louis, and drive to their new home.

And there, thought Ariel several times a day with the odd feeling in the pit of her belly, I shall kiss him on the lips and become Will's wife. Really and truly.

•

After the initial disappointment that he was apparently going to have to wait a bit longer for his kiss, Will enjoyed his birthday. It wasn't hard to read between the lines and guess that Ariel had definite plans for beginning their new life in Gloucester in a meaningful way. He would humour her. And in the meantime, show how much he appreciated the presents she had given him.

The future looked good. Still no nightmares, and not often having any fleeting memory that he was, after all, a murderer. Usually such thoughts came in the middle of the night and he would tell himself he could redeem those wrongs by treating Ariel better – including reclaiming her beloved cats – and wrapped himself more closely around her sleeping form.

He looked forward to their drive back to Whittington. He decided to go east and show her Yorkshire, even though it wasn't the fastest route. He knew she would enjoy seeing the Cow and Calf on the Ilkley Moor they'd been singing about for several weeks. Singing loudly – and hopelessly out of tune – was their current pastime of choice in the car. He amazed himself at the number of old songs whose words he could actually remember, and Ariel picked them up in a flash, the better to join in. And of course there would also be different birds in Yorkshire for her Life List, just as there had been on Skye.

There was no urgency. If they arrived next Monday they could be ready for the movers who were coming on Tuesday. They would load the car; then he would ring Mrs Leeds and collect the cats before they set off for Gloucester on Monday evening. He'd already told the movers where to find the key and what to do with it afterwards. They'd spend that night in their new home – probably sleeping on the floor, but in their own home nonetheless.

•

'Dave, remember that woman you didn't see this summer – the one with the strange bird?' Janice was having one of her irregular phone calls to her brother

'Ariel Pike you mean? Yes, I do remember. There was something about her voice that sort of stays with me. She sounded familiar in a way. Not like I knew her, but…'

'Maybe she sounded like we do – like she came from Norfolk?'

'Yes, that could be it. I hadn't thought of that. Why, anyway?'

'Roger can't get it out of his head that Pike was the last name of that missing girl from Sheringham two or three years ago. He's badgering the inspector to give him permission to take another man with him and check it out. So he needs the address – can you remember it?

'I've got the postcode written down, yes. Hang on.' He found his notebook quickly and gave the details to his sister. 'You guys must not have much to do in the Force these days if Roger can swing a junket like that after all this time.'

'You're a fine one to talk! You went there twice on company time and money!'

'True, Oh Queen. When's he going?'

'He doesn't know. The inspector hasn't said yes, yet. In any case, Rog doesn't really think anything will come from it, but he likes the fantasy of a promotion for trying.'

TWENTY-SIX

The drive from Skye back to the Midlands via Yorkshire was uneventful and quick. It had seemed exciting as they planned it but once they actually set off they became aware – almost in the same moment – that they were really more anxious to get back to Whittington Moor, do the necessary clean up and move on to Gloucester. This part of their life was ending and they were both keen to get started on the next part.

Packing up the remainder of their belongings went smoothly and took far less time than Will had told Ariel to expect. 'It would have gone even faster if you'd kept the towels in their proper order,' he grumbled, but she could tell he wasn't really cross about it. She did better with the sheets and kitchen towels and earned herself a reassuring hug.

They had a final cup of tea before putting the tea things into the car along with whatever else they could cram in to make the first night in their new home more comfortable. 'Save room for the cats' things, please,' Ariel reminded him, more than once.

'Okay. Let's get everything ready to go so that all I have to do is fetch the cats, tuck their box in the back seat, come back and collect you, and away we go.' Ariel had wanted to come with him, but he'd told her he needed her to have one last look around. He didn't mention how difficult Mrs Leeds had been on the telephone about his apparent change of heart, but what the hell. He could be humble and conciliatory with her for a few minutes; he'd never have to see her again. 'Let's have a final hug in this house, and off I'll go.'

She stood as close to him as she could and, standing on her tiptoes with her face turned up to his, reached up to kiss him full on his lips. She realised he was surprised, but recovered himself quickly and responded in such a way that she thought her insides were melting. When he moved slowly and reluctantly away she heard herself give a little moan. She thought he did, too.

'Ariel! Whoa. That was... really something special.' He held her away from him, looking intently into her eyes. 'I... I...

you… bloody hell, I'm lost for words. But thank you!'

She felt wonderful. 'I liked that a lot Will. If that – that sort of thing – is what it's like to be your wife really, then I can hardly wait. Can I be your real wife tonight, do you think? Even though I'm not fourteen yet?'

'Do you know what you are saying?'

She nodded, and reached up to kiss him again. 'I do,' she said solemnly, although she knew she did not.

He laughed. 'That's what marrying couples say. I do. I do too, Ariel! All right! Tonight, then If you're sure.' He suddenly looked worried.

'I'm sure.' She was. That much she did know. She was sure that Will would make it all perfect. One hundred per cent sure. She'd like to say a hundred and ten per cent, except she knew Will would not like that, and she was not going to do anything to spoil this wonderful moment.

'Right then, I'm off to get our children and then away we'll go. One more kiss for the road, please – a quick one, this time.'

She stood at the open door and watched him get into the car, singing 'On Ilkley Moor bar t'at' at the top of his voice. Unusually for him he raced the engine and drove quickly up the drive and out of sight. Her kiss had been spontaneous, after all. And he hadn't locked her in. Ariel hardly had time to realise these two seemingly unrelated thoughts when she heard the crash.

Her first thought was that it might delay Will's getting to Mrs Leeds, but in a split second realised that he was the crash. Almost immediately she could hear voices, people shouting, and for a long moment she couldn't move. Her legs, which didn't seem to belong to her any more, had apparently taken root and were stuck in the ground. In an unsuccessful effort to see more, she leaned as far forward as she could without falling over and put her hand on her heart to try to stop its thumping that was so hard that it actually hurt. Then she found her legs and ran hard up the drive where, in the deepening twilight, she could see the wreck of Will's car and another one, a massive four-wheel drive thing, almost buried in the side of his. A man – the driver of the other car? – was talking on his mobile phone and another one was sitting on the side of the road, crying loudly. She couldn't see Will. She couldn't even see where he ought to be sitting, in the driver's seat. That side of the car was completely smashed in.

She stood at the end of their driveway holding onto their wooden post box, staring in bewilderment and horror as two women got out of the back of the other car to join the man on the side of the road. The three of them huddled together, moaning and crying. Nobody seemed to notice her and she had a sudden thought that if she simply stood there long enough, postman Harry would eventually come along and maybe make it all right. He would give her the post and she would take it to Will.

Will. Where was he? She couldn't see him. Dare she call out for him? Maybe he was on the other side of the tangled smash. Maybe he was sitting on the side of the road, waiting for her but out of sight. He couldn't be in the car. It wasn't possible for anyone to be in what was left of their car.

She could hear sirens and then saw the flashing lights of the emergency vehicles: a fire engine, two police cars, an ambulance, one after the other. Men piled out of them and swarmed around the wreck, talking and shouting: the noise was unbearable. She put her fingers in her ears.

After what seemed both an age and no time at all, one of the police officers noticed her. He came over to her and stood between her and the wrecked cars. 'All right love? Did you see what happened?' She shook her head and tried to move around him, the better to see what the men were doing. He moved too, continuing to block her view. 'I shouldn't look if I were you, my love. It's not a nice sight.'

She found her voice. 'Is… is he all right?'

'Who, sweetheart? The people from the SUV seem to be all right. A bit shaken up, as you'd expect. Their vehicle's gone straight through the passenger side and demolished the whole front of the blue car. That man's dead, I'm afraid.' He looked at her. 'Do you have any idea who he is?'

The world spun round her, the red and blue lights flashing in her eyes and slicing into her brain. She pushed the policeman's hands away and clung to the post box, willing Harry to show up and make everything all right. Then the noise suddenly stopped and the world stood still again. Ice-cold blood flooded her body and she felt her legs giving way just as the policeman put his arms around her waist to hold her up. She screwed her hands into tight fists and hit at his chest, trying to push him away, trying to make him let go so she could get to Will. She opened her mouth to tell him to let her go and heard herself scream, 'It's Will! He's my dad! He's my DAD!'

TWENTY-SEVEN

'So how are you and your dad getting along, Ariel?'

Despite the unfamiliar and somewhat grating Geordie accent, and the apparently endless supply of layered, multi-coloured floating chiffon scarves, she didn't really dislike this counsellor: Rosie. She wasn't as pushy and nosey as some and she'd been the first – actually the only – person to ask her if she'd like to be called Ariel.

After a bewildering series of interviews, examinations and sessions with a never-ending stream of policemen, doctors, psychiatrists and social workers – to say nothing of foster carers – this had felt like such a gift that Ariel felt she wanted to give something back.

'It's all right,' listlessly.

Rosie waited.

Ariel moistened her lips and took a breath, 'In some ways.'

'Do you want to talk about the ways that it is all right, or the ways it isn't all right?'

Neither, really. But, 'Well... he's... he's not... I mean, he's...'

'He's not Will?'

Ariel shrugged and shook her head.

'And you're really missing Will.'

And how! Will was the only person in the world who could have helped her cope with all she'd had to cope with lately. Except he wasn't 'in the world' any more, and that was the problem.

The emergency foster carer she'd been taken to on that awful night had seemed worried at first that Ariel might not believe that Will had been killed and wasn't coming back. Oh she'd believed all right, right from the moment the fat policeman had told her she couldn't stay by herself at the house and she'd asked him if she could go home with him.

'We'll see,' he'd said, and moved away from her. She knew that in this case it meant no, and wondered why she'd thought, even for a nano-second, that he might be at least a temporary replacement dad.

She and Will had made a pact a long time ago never to say 'we'll see'. As an obfuscating tactic (she loved that word and had used it several times a day for weeks after Will introduced her to it) 'we'll see' had been part of her mother's armoury for many years, and she'd hated it. Before Will; BW, as he would say, but BD (before Dad) is how she privately thought of it. They had discussed how dishonest it was and what a waste of energy it was to have to work out whether it meant yes, no or I don't know yet, and – this was always the best part of such discussions – had made a list together of possible replacements as well as times when it could actually be perfectly acceptable as a response.

'What's the weather going to be like tomorrow, Ariel?' he'd offer, and 'We'll see,' she'd say cheekily, and like as not he'd ruffle her hair or pull a face at her. Or both. She missed times like that.

Susan and Geoff, the first foster carers she was taken to, did their best. Susan chattily and uncomplainingly delivered her to her various appointments with doctors and social workers, and Geoff volunteered to take her to the pet shop to buy her a goldfish. A goldfish! The very idea that a cold-blooded object like a goldfish could replace her warm and loving Will – or her warm and loving cats, for that matter – made her feel sick.

As did all the questions. The police were the worst. The hatchet-faced sergeant's, 'Did he interfere with you, sweetheart?' staggered her. Interfere! What a word to use to describe what was going to happen – in love – that night, if only Will hadn't shot across the road without looking properly. If only the other car hadn't been barrelling down their road. If only it had damaged just the passenger side and not gone right through and crushed Will. If only she'd been with him so they could have died together and she wouldn't have to deal with all this. If only she hadn't distracted him by kissing him in such a grown-up way. If only. If only. The if-only's were endless. The counsellor told her they were a normal part of grieving and for a moment, when she said that, explaining about stages of grief, Ariel thought how much she and Will would have enjoyed making one of their endless set of lists; this time of the stages and documenting together what happened each day and into which stage it would fit. Such research and explorations had been the meat and drink of their days together. She missed times like that, too.

The policewoman evidently hadn't believed her desolate headshake and had delivered her up for the most embarrassing, intrusive and humiliating ninety minutes of her life with their medical officer. He, watched the entire time by the female sergeant, felt her all over, took photographs of her breasts and genitals, and stuck his fingers and what looked like the things Will had showed her how to clean her ears with into places she didn't even know she had.

'Did he touch you here?' Sullen head shake. 'Here?' The same. 'How about here?' And on, and on, and on. No, no, NO! What's the matter with you twisted people? Will would never have done things that you are doing.

At one point she muttered, 'No, but Jock did,' but they seemed not to hear it.

She'd even had a visit from Dave from the BTO. She had looked forward to that, hoping they could discuss birds, Will's Life List, and anything else that would help her feel closer again to the absent Will. He'd arrived with yet another policeman – Detective Sergeant Aston this time – and it was quickly obvious that his only purpose in being there was to help the police pin something, anything, she didn't know what, on Will. The disappointment was so great and his excitement that he had seen her hoopoe, so out of place now, that she had cried longer and harder after that meeting than at any other time before or since.

After Susan and Geoff ('we are only temporary, emergency carers, you see') she'd gone to a residential youth care home in Burton. There were two other girls her age, and a boy of eleven. They gave her a room of her own, but she was encouraged – no, urged – to spend very little time in there. She was supposed to 'engage' with the girls, which apparently meant talking about boys, clothes and make up, watching dull things on television, and occasionally nicking a lipstick or a Mars Bar from the local Spar. One of them had offered her a strange-looking tablet she said she'd got from her boyfriend, and both of them, together and separately, had urged her to sniff and suck on the nozzle of a hairspray can. She'd shaken her head, confused, somehow sensing this was not a journey she wanted to begin, and especially not with them.

Even if she'd wanted to connect with them, her despair – cold and brittle, and filling all the spaces in her body – kept her separate. She knew, without knowing how or why she knew, that her experience with Will had set her outside any expectations of a normal relationship with her peers.

At first she'd wanted to talk about Will and what their life together had been like, but they didn't listen. Or if they did, they had been so uncomprehending that she had quickly given up.

But they'd evidently taken in more than she'd realised, and passed on what they'd heard to the manager of the house who, on learning about the system of symbols on Will's calendar, and observing Ariel's car-counting activities and her insistence on putting clean things under the neat stack already in the drawers, had taken Ariel to a psychiatrist to see if she had something she called OCD. Ariel thought she had talked her way out of it – 'it was his thing really; I just did it to make life easier all round'. She thought it better not to say that actually, she found these activities quite soothing, especially during the past few horrendous weeks, and that she could quite see Will's point, but the experience convinced her that another defence from early childhood was her only possible course from now on: When you don't know what to say, or you don't know how what you say will be received, say nothing. They can't get you for that. Well, to be fair, Jock did get her for that, but she wasn't living with Jock any more, so silence was a safer bet. Silence was also quite powerful, she discovered.

After a series of mostly silent interviews with the Special Needs person from the Burton School District, she was sent, briefly, to the nearest secondary school. It had been brief because the gaps in her basic educational knowledge were so huge, but the amount of knowledge of so many other, more esoteric, things was so astonishing, that they simply – and they said so – didn't know what to do with her. She said nothing, silently observing to herself that they went in for a lot of hyperbole and litotes, not to mention periphrasis, when dealing with her. Something else she would have enjoyed communicating with Will about. He'd only recently introduced these particular definitions and he always seemed to enjoy it when she demonstrated her understanding of such concepts. She didn't like school, finding many lessons incomprehensible and others so unbelievably simplistic that she spent long periods in the toilets, desperately trying to stop crying. Arrangements would be made, they said, for her to have private tutoring of some kind, to bring her up to speed so that she could return to mainstream education. She alternated between dreading that and hoping the tutor would be someone she could admire and really talk with. A man, preferably. A fatherly type.

Perhaps because she hadn't been to formal school for over two years, the social worker she saw twice a week during her time in Burton talked to her as if she were still about eight or nine. She, too, was very interested in how and when Will had 'interfered' with her, and would invite Ariel to play with the puppets to show what life with Will had been like on a daily basis. Ariel would say nothing, so the social worker – Chrissie, this time, who always wore long flowery skirts in what to Ariel were extremely unpleasant colour combinations – would put the ugly brown dog and the revolting yellowish duckling onto her lap, interpreting Ariel's tears of despair as evidence that they were on the right track. During one of her many sleepless nights, Ariel thought if she didn't feel so completely empty and weary, it might actually be amusing to see what 'evidence' she could plant for Chrissie's interpretation. But no, the truth was Will had loved her and nurtured her in every possible way, and taken wonderful care of her for the entire time they had been together. They'd had fun together, too. Why couldn't anyone get that?

The first counsellor, at Burton, had been a disaster. Ariel had forgotten her name. She had been dumpy and middle-aged, and had smelled much the same as Miss at primary school had. Ariel had forgotten her name too. Mentally she thanked Will for teaching her to forget things she didn't want to remember.

The Burton counsellor had hardly bothered to hide her disapproval of Will.

'He was not a good man, Jessie. He broke the law by abducting you.'

'He didn't abduct me. I went with him of my own accord. I wanted to be with him.' Like I don't want to be with you, she thought. Therefore quite possibly you could be said to be breaking the law?

The counsellor had ignored her reply. 'It's against the law to have sex with a minor – which you were and still are.'

'He didn't have sex with me.'

'Jessie, the investigators have your journal. We know you slept together.'

'Well then, you'll know that we didn't have sex. We only slept together, which is what I wrote about.' Ariel tried and failed to quell the triumphant note.

The counsellor smiled sadly. 'People are known to be untruthful in journals, alas.'

'So how do you know that I wasn't lying about sleeping together then? How do you know I wasn't making that up?' Ariel's head was on fire inside, she was so angry. If the counsellor had replied she hadn't heard her. Nor did she speak to that one ever again. Which, when she thought about it, gave her a small sense of power once more.

Eventually it had been decided that the best solution was for Ariel to go to Hexham and live with her father who had been down to Burton several times to spend time with her. His visits hadn't gone badly, and Ariel thought living with him couldn't possibly be worse than staying where she was. After all, she thought wryly, this whole thing had started with her running away to find him. She saw the irony in this; she'd set out to find her dad and had accidentally found something far and away better. And now he'd found her, so she was living with him and his new partner, Ellen.

It was all right. They didn't bombard her with questions or push her into activities she didn't want to do. They encouraged her to continue bird watching and expressed interest in what she had seen – which wasn't much, because Ariel had no appetite for it without Will. At first Ellen was happy to play Monopoly or

Scrabble with her, but was so hopeless at both that Ariel quickly gave up. As for Killer Sudoku, you'd have thought she was trying to explain Chinese hieroglyphics to them, they were so head-shakingly bemused when she showed them how she did it. She decided not to mention cryptic crosswords.

They'd started by calling her Jessie, but lately had changed to Jessica, which she didn't like at all. Yet somehow she didn't want them to call her Ariel, so after some thought, decided not to argue about it. She had begun her life without Will by vehemently protesting when everyone but Rosie called her Jessie: 'It's ARIEL', but eventually gave up in despair. Nobody listened to her.

One of the social workers had told her that she wouldn't be returning to her mother and another one had told her that David had been taken into care and could eventually end up with their father too. That might be all right, too, she thought, although they didn't know each other at all any more and their brief meetings in Burton had been strained and uncomfortable. He'd seemed rather more like Jock than the naïve and innocent little brother she remembered. She supposed that she and he both had moved on over the years they'd been apart, albeit in very different directions.

The visit with Milly had been difficult, too. The social worker (Amy, Chrissie, Sarah – most of the time Ariel couldn't tell them apart and in any case didn't want to bother) had warned Ariel that her mother might be angry, or distant and withdrawn, and that Ariel should be prepared to make conversation. In the event, Milly had prattled almost non-stop.

'Ooh, you look so different! Doesn't she?' appealing to the social worker.

'I think that's probably to be expected, Mrs Pike,' the social worker had smiled encouragingly. 'You haven't seen her for nearly two years.'

'You don't,' Ariel had said.

'Don't I? I've had my hair done though. And my nails as well – look! I couldn't decide on gold or the sparkly green, what do you think? Do you like these shoes? I got them specially to come today. They're killing me, I have to say.'

There had been no need – or space – for Ariel to reply, so she simply sat still, reading and rereading the social workers' diplomas that hung on the walls around the room, rubbing her finger up and down the arm of the chair, and waited for the visit to be over.

'I'll be seeing you again soon, our Jessie,' Milly burbled. 'Maybe we can go shopping or on some outings together. We've got to get to know each other again. We thought you was dead. Ooh, I've missed you so much.' To Ariel's horror, her mother began to cry, messily.

'We'll see. I'll be in touch soon. Thank you for coming Mrs Pike.'

Briefly Ariel was grateful for the intervention and tried to show it by smiling at the social worker who said, when the door had closed behind Milly, 'How was that for you, Jessie?'

The gratitude faded.

'All right,' dully. 'Do I have to see her again?'

'Well… no, I suppose not if you don't want to, we'll have to see. But don't make any decisions yet, see how you feel in a week or so.'

Ariel could not then have put it into words, but the gulf between where she had been, what she'd had with Will, and the sort of life Milly was inviting her back in to, was so vast that her brain felt as if it were simply shutting down. She shook her head.

•

'I don't know. I don't know what I want to do.'

Ariel had asked various people about Jock but for the most part had received only irritatingly obfuscating responses. She couldn't be sure, but she thought he might have been arrested and even jailed for something, but no one was going to confirm or deny it for her, always rapidly changing the subject whenever she brought it up. David had hinted at it, though Ariel could tell he'd been under orders not to say anything. At least that hadn't changed: she could still read him like a book, she thought, and not really a very interesting book at that.

Most distressing was the lack of information about Will. She sensed very quickly that in the official view he had done something terribly wrong and that everything about his life, and their life together, was being investigated. But nobody would tell her anything, fobbing her off with responses like: 'Don't you worry about all that, that's all over; your job now is to get on with your life.' As if she could, as if she had a life now Will was gone.

In a way, she didn't want to know what was being said about him. She knew a lot of it would be lies; they simply wouldn't understand his much higher motives or their work to continue what the Durants had started. She felt totally unable to defend him or repair his reputation, so after a while she stopped asking and chose not to look at newspapers or listen to radio or TV news, or even to Google him. She knew that whatever she read or heard would make her feel ill.

Another social worker had talked to her about the need for her to be 'looked after now'. This both puzzled and infuriated her; she had never in her life felt as 'looked after' as she had with Will. At the Burton home – and even with her father and Ellen – she experienced huge gaps in the care she had come to expect and relish from Will. They all fed and clothed her well, as had Will, but the mental stimulation, the ever-challenging and exciting conversation, the shared jokes and discoveries, were now negligible to non-existent.

She missed Will, but even more, she missed the experience of being with Will. And in her most desolate moments she knew without any doubt that she would never have such an experience again. At such times she was beyond tears; she was simply numb.

•

In the long silence since the counsellor had asked if she'd rather talk about what was all right or what was not, she'd sat perfectly still, chewing her lower lip and staring into space as her mind drifted back to random memories of times with Will. Going swimming at Tamworth Baths, getting her own bird book and binoculars, his giving her a drink of chocolate at their first meeting, naming the cats Louis and Ethel, roller skating and making a cake for his birthday and, on Skye, cooking for him and pretending to be his wife. The memories were endless, and the pain of them was unbearable.

'"One person is missing and the world is empty",' she whispered.

'Sorry?'

'It's a quote,' flatly. 'Keats, I think, but I'm not sure. Will would know, of course he would, he told me it.'

'He taught you a lot, didn't he?'

She nodded, suddenly becoming aware that she was crying, again, and evidently had been for quite a while, judging by the dampness on the front of her jumper.

'Our love was like sunshine, like a rainbow. It coloured everything near it.'

'That's very poetic, Ariel'.

She knew Rosie was trying to be complimentary, but she also knew that she didn't really understand. Ariel decided – again – to say less, possibly even nothing.

'Maybe you'd like to talk about Will?'

'Well, I might,' Ariel was instantly suspicious. 'But not if you're going to ask if he "interfered" with me and things like that, because he didn't and I'm tired of saying that. He was the most wonderful person in the world and would never have done anything to harm me.'

'I know he didn't, Ariel. I know he loved you and I know you loved him. And I know you can't imagine how you're going to go on living without him. I also know that talking about someone we've lost can often be really helpful.'

'Will never wanted to talk about people he'd lost. I don't think he thought it would be helpful.'

Rosie tilted her head to the side and raised one eyebrow slightly.

'No? Who didn't he want to talk about, Ariel?'

'Nobody.' Ariel flinched inwardly at Rosie's sudden interest in what Will thought and decided instantly that it would not be safe to talk about him and what he would or wouldn't talk about to her. Crikey! Will had told her that it was better to forget about some things, and what better way to forget than to simply not talk about them?

Maybe she could even forget that Will had died. That was the absolute ultimate in things she didn't want to remember. How proud of her Will would be if she could forget that.

She took a deep shuddering breath and felt her spirits lift a little as the thought occurred that forgetting he had died, and refusing to discuss Will with anyone, including Rosie, would be a way she could actually be like Will.

She smiled a little smile and closed her eyes, imagining his face as he looked approvingly at her newfound confidence. She was vaguely aware that Rosie was speaking to her, asking or telling her something, but she felt no need to respond. She stayed silent, eyes closed, clinging to the vision of Will's gently smiling face, and vowing to be as much like him as she possibly could. She counted the cars as they passed Rosie's window: Two-one to Hexham, three-one to Hexham, three-two, three-all... Maybe she'd start charting the counts, recording and comparing different times of day and different days of the week. Will would have been pleased with that; it was the sort of thing he liked doing himself. She'd get herself a calendar and come up with a symbol for, say, most cars to Hexham in one counting period.

TWENTY-EIGHT

The fantasy of becoming more and more like Will grew as she walked home from Rosie's clinic. Ideas tumbled in and out of her brain almost making her feel dizzy. She could change her name (to what though?). She could get the crossword and Sudoku online as he'd always done. She would work harder at getting to grips with Walt Whitman; Will had admired him and had been a bit disappointed that she'd never quite taken to his poetry. She would ask her dad and Ellen if she could have Will's library of the Durants' writings and if she couldn't, she'd ask for them for Christmas. Or buy them herself – she'd have no compunction about stealing whatever money was necessary to do that. She could find a new apprentice-Ariel to instruct in philosophy, and the Durants' way of thinking and being. Maybe David, if he came to live with them, would like to learn the things Will had taught her. Maybe she would stay Ariel and change David's name to Will. No, no—to Louis; he could be her adopted son and she could continue as the widowed Ariel. No, that wouldn't be right because the original Ariel had died first and Will had lived only a few days longer, such was his grief. Or had it been the other way round, and Will had died first? At any rate, they had died within days of each other.

Should she die, and complete the circle that way? She wasn't keen and fancied she could feel her Will telling her that would be wrong. No, he said quite clearly in her mind, it was her responsibility to stay here and continue their work.

But how? The euphoria dipped a little, but rose again as she thought of asking the Will in her head and feeling fairly sure that somehow he would answer. He hadn't believed in any kind of life after death, or communicating with the departed, so of course Ariel couldn't expect he would actually answer her questions. But seeing his face in her mind's eye when she realised what Rosie was up to, ferreting for information, gave her the confidence to believe that she would be able to do that again, perhaps at will, and that he would somehow communicate his approval or suggestions in that way.

At will. At Will! What a nice phrase, she thought with a smile, as she opened the front door and went inside. Still smiling, she climbed the stairs, went into her room and sat at the computer where she Googled 'Will and Ariel Durant'.

•••

About the Author

Margaret Pitz has been writing stories in her head for as long as she can remember. This is her first published novel.

Also by the Author

After Dad **(2014)**

A coming-of-age story with a difference, **After Dad** is the story of Ariel (formerly Jessie Pike) and her emergence into the world after spending two years as the often-willing abductee of Will, a man whose fantasy required the two of them to become two other people entirely. This is the story of her emotional healing and re-entry into normal life as she absorbs and comes to terms with the horror of what happened to her in those two missing years.

Alice in Madland **(2015)**

It's 1958 and 17-year-old Alice Chorley's career aspirations are in tatters. She takes a mindless office job where she is drawn into – and colludes with – the mad fantasy world of senior secretary Pearl Taylor. Their 'Game' is played out in counterpoint to Alice's more normal (though unsatisfactory) relationship with her boyfriend, Jack. The fantasies escalate and the tension mounts, leading to an explosive confrontation, a startling revelation and, ultimately, a different life for Alice.

Praise for *Finding Dad*

"Full of insight, humanity and suspense, it offers much food for thought . . . an unusual, uneasy, even shocking read, skilfully told by an author who enters the minds of her characters and brings them to life on the pages." (Reviews: Amazon.co.uk)

www.ingramcontent.com/pod-product-compliance
Lightning Source LLC
Chambersburg PA
CBHW060823120626
46557CB00001B/346